The Assassin's Identity

Written by Joseph Ganci Sr.

Dedication

I dedicate this book to my loving wife Joan who has supported my efforts and passion for the arts our entire life together. Her patience, love, and devotion in being my soul mate for life has sustained and nurtured me and our four children Diane, Susan, Joseph Jr., and Michael in all the good times and bad.

CHAPTER 1   THE RECALL TO DUTY

The sun rises and reflects over the clear blue waters of the keys, as Michael walks out of his beach shack for his morning stroll. He walks slowly down the white sandy beach to take in the cool morning air, as he has done every morning for the past year. Suddenly the sound of a black helicopter breaks the silence of the morning and lowers onto the beach 50 yards adjacent to his shack and where he is walking.

Michael stands their surprised as two men in black jump suits emerge from the copter and run towered him. He noticed that the markings on the helicopter had the red NWO 13 marking in red on its side. He knew immediately that it was the agency in pursuit. One of the men was carrying a small black brief case and the other a small arms weapon.

When they reached about 50 ft from Michael the one with the brief case threw it at Michael's feet. They then both turned and ran back to the helicopter, got in, and the bird lifted and out of sight. Michael stood there dumb founded and watched them depart. He then fetched the brief case and returned quickly with it to his shack. He thought (My year of solitude and peace has now come to an end.)

He sat down at his kitchen table, opened the black briefcase, and emptied its contents on the table. There are two letters, a pack of $100 bills, a silver pistol with a silencer, a box of bullets and two new passports, one Ukrainian and one Russian. He opened the first envelope and pulled out a blank piece of paper folded up and two pictures. Michael knew that he had to us his special invisible ink restore solution to read the message. He went into his bedroom and retrieved a small black case from the top shelf of his closet. He then proceeded to apply the solution to the blank piece of paper and revealed the message.

It read " Michael the pictures are of two Russian Oligarchs located in New York city. They are both Russian spies and are residing in the Russian Diplomatic Compound building in the Bronx, which Houses the Russian diplomats and spies. They have diplomatic immunity so we can't apprehend them or deport them. They are very dangerous characters and have attempted to infiltrate an important governmental research company on Long Island. They must be eliminated.

We are calling on you because it must look like an accident and your resourcefulness is essential. The address of the building is 355 West 255th street in River dale, Bronx. One cannot get access to the inside of the building because it is guarded. We have also enclosed a picture of their car and license plates. They park them in the garage below the building, Good luck, signed Chief."

Michael then opened the second envelope, and it was a letter from Cynthia. It read "Dear white rose I have missed you terribly for the past year and don't know if you are dead or alive or if this letter will ever get to you. I passed in on to Rossard and asked him to get it to you if possible. If you are OK and can travel to Europe, send me a note at the Vineyard. Cyn."

Michael sat back in his chair sighed and stared into space. He realized that his life in seclusion was no longer his preference. He missed both the intrigue of his clandestine activities and his encounter with Cynthia. He made himself a perfect Manhattan on the rocks, lifted his glass pointed it to the letter and down it. He then packed his regular clothes, shaved, took a shower and prepared to leave his shack on the beach. It was time to give up his cut down jeans.

The next morning, he closed and locked up his shack called a cab to take him from the Key's to Miami airport. The first thing he did was to arrange for a florist in Paris to send a long white stem rose with a note to Cynthia. " I'm OK miss you too very much. I will be in touch soon. Michael"

Arriving at Miami airport he boarded a plane for LaGuardia airport in New York. hours later he then took a cab to Manhattan and to the park lane hotel near Central Park. He settled into a suite overlooking the park, which had all the amenities of a great hotel. It was in walking distance to the park, which afforded him the opportunity of taking a morning run through the park.

Although he was not keen on carrying out another assassination mission, he realized it must be important and had to do it. (But how he thought?) He spent the next few days raking the subway to the Bronx, casing the building and surroundings. He realized that there was a security guard posted at the entrance of the garage who checked credentials for people driving their cars into the garage. He sat in his car across the street and watched demonstrators against the war in Ukraine and to see if one of his targets would drive out or in.

After three days of surveillance one of the cars matching the license plate in his picture emerged from the garage and drove off. He followed the car all the way to long Island where it parked outside a restaurant. The guy got out and entered the restaurant and met with some woman for lunch. Michael saw his opportunity and casually walked over to the guy's car and placed a small explosive device on the left front wheel of the car and walked back to his car and waited.

About an hour later the guy left the restaurant got in his car and drove off. Michael followed him to the Long Island thruway and at a precarious turn off, Michael pressed the button on his cell phone. The device placed on the car exploded and the car swerved off the road and over an embankment into a ditch smoking. It caught fire and the driver was killed instantly. Michael drove off, speeding back to Manhattan and his hotel. When he arrived, he went straight to the cocktail Lounge and got himself a Perfect Bourbon Manhattan on the rocks.

The following day the New York times had an article that said a Russian diplomat was killed by a motor accident on the Long Island thruway. It described the accident as the car went out of control and over the embankment. Michael thought (One down, one to go.) He also read that the other guy had been expelled and was leaving the US on a plane for Warsaw Poland the following day. Michael knew the guy was carrying information that he would be delivering to the Russian Embassy in Warsaw and then make his way back to Russia. He had to stop him from getting away.

CHAPTER 2 WARSAW POLAND

The following day early in the morning, Michael checked out of the hotel and caught a taxi to LaGuardia airport. He waited at the international travel terminal and outside the check in counter of Canadian Airlines because they had the most flights to Warsaw. His hunch paid off and his target arrived and walked over the check in counter. Michael quickly followed him and booked a first-class seat on the same flight.

He was able to board the plane first and sat in a seat up front and watched as the passengers entered the plane, one by one. As he thought would happen his target also entered early and sat in a seat across from him in first class. The guy took a small carry-on bag and stored it in the bin on top. He had a small black leather brief case which he held at his feet.

The flight attendant entered the cabin to take drink orders from the first-class passengers. Michael asked for a Bourbon on the rocks and the target asked for a vodka on the rocks. Michael noticed that the guy seemed very nervous and downed is drink fast and asked for another. The flight attendant obliged and brought him another quickly. Michael sipped his drink and took a while before he finished it. By this time the plane had reached its cruising altitude of about 50,000 feet. Since it was a long flight, Michael had time to figure out how he would get hold of the contents of the little black briefcase that the target was carrying.

Michael struck up a conversation with the guy and exchanged pleasantries. The guy asked him why he was traveling to Poland. "I am a vehicle parts dealer, and I am meeting to sell them to Poland. What about you?" The guy responded that he was on his way to return from a diplomatic assignment." Michael was surprised at his candor and arrogance and thought (This guy must be very confident about his ability to carry out his plan.)

Since it was a transatlantic flight, they served a meal on the flight. Michael ordered a red wine with his meal, but the other guy ordered another vodka with his. The flight lasted about eleven hours and Michael had time to plan how he would get his hands on the black briefcase his target was carrying.

In the middle of the flight the Russian fell asleep and still had half a drink on his tray. Michael got up and went to the bathroom where he pulled out of his pocket a small vial of fluid containing a knockout drug. On his return to his seat the lights on the plane are in a dim mode because. When he reached the seat, he poured the drops into the guy's drink to ensure he would stay asleep for the next couple of hours.

Michael waited patiently while the guy awoke, took a drink and fell back into a deep sleep. Michael waited for an opportune moment while everything was quiet and dark, and he reached over and grabbed the black briefcase. He used his training skills to jimmy the lock, open it and take out all the papers. he put them in his brief case and replaced them with the flight magazine, closed the case and replaced it at the feet of the Russian.

Hours later the plane landed at the Chopin airport in Warsaw Poland. Michael immediately went to the baggage area and waited as the baggage was being unloaded. He stood near the Russian diplomat as they waited for their luggage. Michael purposely brushed against the guy and stuck him with a small pin laced with a time release poison, which would take about two hours to produce a heart attack. He then grabbed his bag and walked briskly away.

Michael caught a taxi and went directly to the American Embassy where he reported to the resident CIA chief that he had accomplished his mission and he turned over papers from the Russian's briefcase. They reviewed the obfuscated papers and were surprised and thankful that Michael was able to stop them from getting in the hands of the Russian embassy. While they were still in the conference room an aid to the chief came into the room and reported that a radio broadcast stated that a Russian diplomat had died of a heart attack in a taxi on his way to the Russian Embassy. They all looked at Michael and smiled. They all knew it was Michael's accomplishment.

The station chief told everyone to leave the room except for Michael who was requested to stay. When they left, he turned to Michael and said, "We have another special sensitive assignment for you." Michael leaned his elbows on the table and listened carefully. Michael there is Russian Oligarch that is close to the top of the Russian leaders in Moscow. He is a multi-billionaire and a CEO of a Russian oil company. He has taken his mega yacht to the island of Montenegro to avoid it being seized by the authorities. Russian assets were being seized where possible, due to the invasion of Russia in Ukraine.

The ship has stopped sending tracking signals, but it is believed it is headed for Tivat. We need you to try and locate it, board it, and force the captain to the port of Mallorca. There the 300-million-dollar yacht will be seized. If the owner is aboard, then you are to eliminate him before it gets to port. This will take all your cunning an experience and could be dangerous.

After his verbal briefing, Michael was handed an envelope with pictures of the Oligarch, his yacht, plane tickets for business class from Warsaw to Tivat Montenegro for the next morning. He left the meeting and went straight to a hotel near the airport where he would be spending the night. He checked in and then went straight to the cocktail lounge for his afternoon perfect Bourbon Manhattan on the rocks. A half hour later he returned to his room, watched some TV, and then ordered room service of a steak dinner with a carafe of red wine. After eating his dinner, he sat and relaxed reviewed the contents of the envelope again. He then retired for a good night's sleep.

CHAPTER 3   Tivat Montenegro

Michael rose at five AM from a deep sleep when his phone rang with his wake-up call. He took a quick shower, made himself a cup of coffee with his room amenity, dressed and went down to the lobby with his bags to check out. He took the courtesy car to the airport to catch his 6: 25 AM Lufthansa flight. He went straight to boarding gate and was able to bypass the regular security check with his diplomatic credentials.

When he settled into his seat, the blonde attractive flight attendant asked him if she could get him anything. He responded with "Yes thank you. Can you bring me a cup of coffee and a pastry?" " Yes, sir and I will be serving you breakfast when we reach our cruising altitude." "Thank you" Sure enough when the plane reached about 50,000 Feet, returned with a tray with a breakfast tray of orange Juice, coffee, an assortment of German bread and marmalade, and slices of cold cuts.

The flight was about 11 hours, had one stop in Frankfurt and then proceeded on to Tivat. It allowed him to catch twenty winks, was served a hot lunch steak, potatoes, red cabbage. He also was given a choice of red or white wine. There was also a small apple strudel for desert on his tray. The long flight was uneventful and smooth, and the attractive attendant helped make it pleasurable. He kept thinking about different scenarios on he would complete his upcoming task and his typical anxiety kicked in for a while. As in the past he learned to overcome it with a special breathing exercise.

When he landed in the Tivat Montenegro airport, he took a taxi to the Regent Porto Montenegro hotel. He checked in to a Deluxe Sea view room that overlooked the Adriatic Sea and a large Marina on Boca Bay. From his balcony he could see a large mega yacht docked at the end of the Marina on the left pf the dock. He proceeded to check out the hotel and found it be truly a five-star facility. He was pleased to find out that there are three cocktail lounges and a great restaurant, a fitness center and a great pool with lounge chairs facing the bay.

He left the hotel and took a walk down the long walkway of the Marina to check out the yacht parked at the end of the dock. Sure enough, it is the one he was asked to find. He returned to the hotel and went to the library bar for his perfect Bourbon Manhattan on the rocks. He ordered a snack of Montenegro cheese selection of goat's cheese, with marinated olives. He sat there enjoying his afternoon libation and observed two young attractive women enjoying their afternoon drink. He quickly realized that they were speaking in Russian. Shortly after they were joined by an elderly gray-haired man. Michael thought (Wow that is the guy he is after.)

While luck would have it, it seems that Montenegro has detained the Yacht and joined the sanctioning of Russian assets. The target was very upset, downed his drink and then walked off. The Two women looked at one another and one shrugged her shoulders as if in disbelief.

Since the Yacht was detained by the authorities, part of Michael's mission was taken care of. He notified his contact back in Warsaw so they could start the seizing of the asset. Now it was time for his plan to eliminate his target. Michael followed the seemly distraught Russian as he traveled straight to Ministry of International affairs office to register a complaint.

Michael waited for the Oligarch to leave the Ministry and then he followed him back to his yacht. Although the yacht was detained pending seizure the Russian thought he might be able persuade the captain to leave the dock that evening before it was seized.

As the sun went down over the Boca Bay, Michael walked slowly to the Yacht entrance that was being guarded by a Russian crewman. He pulled out his silencer under his jacket and pumped two bullets into the guard. He then pulled the fallen body over to the side of the dock and pushed it into the water. He then quickly boards the boat and went straight to the top deck where the Oligarch was trying to convince the captain to announce to the crew to prepare to leave.

Michael shot the Oligarch and then shot the captain. He took the captain's side arm and placed it in the captain's hand. He then made his way down the stairs and off the boat and sprinted back to the Hotel. He headed straight for one of the cocktail Lounges and ordered himself a perfect Bourbon Manhattan on the rocks. After the two of them he then went to the hotel Murano Restaurant to eat dinner. He ordered himself an appetizer of deep-fried Calamari and creamy Polenta with spinach and raisins. Australian Jacks Creek" Rib eye served with potatoes and Croat ruffles, local red wine and for dessert he ordered a Key Lime pie and coffee.

The Following day the local newspaper and TV Broadcast had an expose the speculated that someone had quacked the Russians. They speculated that a disgruntle Ukrainian crewman had taken revenge of the Russian invasion of Ukraine. This was plausible since a week before a Ukrainian crewman had been arrested for attempting to blow up the ship. Michael hung around for a couple more days until the dust settled and then decided that he would make his way back to Warsaw.

Chapter 4   Back in Warsaw

Michael packed up his belongings and caught a taxi to take him to the airport. He then booked a flight on Air France. The Flight had a stay over in Paris for about six hours, so he decided book a hotel room near the airport for the night. He sent a message to Cynthia with a white Rose to tell her he would like her to meet him at the Marriott Airport hotel for a drink and dinner. His cell phone immediately rang. He answered it and Cynthia said "I will be there, happy to know she is OK and did not forget me. Miss you."

Hours later Michael entered the lobby of the hotel to check in and there waiting for him was Cynthia. She ran to him and hugged him and gave him a big kiss. She followed him to his deluxe room and when Michael put his small silver case with his clandestine paraphernalia in the safe, he threw his garment bag on the bed, grabbed Cynthia and gave her another hug and kiss and said, "let's go for a drink." He led her to the cocktail lounge here they sat and chatted for an hour while they sipped their cocktails. They then moved on to the hotel Le Trivium restaurant for dinner. They ordered Foie Gras with seasonal Chutney and nuts, Grilled lamb chop with "Fre Gola Sarda" risotto. Creme Brule for desert and knocked off a bottle of St. Emilion Grand Cru.

During dinner Cynthia asked Michael when he would feel free to pursue the future with, he. He hesitated to tell her the truth and that he was deeply committed to a life of excitement and intrigue. He made her a false promise to satisfy her for the moment.

They left the restaurant, and he led her to his hotel suite. Waiting there was a bucket of ice with a bottle of Champaign and a box of chocolate covered strawberries. He popped the cork and poured two glasses. He lifted his glass and said here's to the two of us. He then grabbed her and took her to his bed, and they made love for an hour.

Finally, she then said "Michael, I have to go." "OK Cyn I have an early flight in the morning anyway and it's just as well." "When will I see you again Michael?" "I don't know, this trip will be a long one" Cynthia left and entered her private car, which was waiting for her, and Michael retired to get a few hours' sleep.

The following morning, he was awakened by a wakeup call at four AM. He showered, dressed, and went to the lobby to check out and catch the shuttle to the airport. He boarded business class on Air France flight that was from Paris nonstop to Warsaw.

Two hours later he got off the plane and picked up his bags and caught a cab to take him to the Hotel Bristol in Odessa. He checked in to a standard room, took his bags and threw them on the bed. He took his small clandestine case and placed it in the safe.

The hotel is only 1.5 km from the railway station, and 1 km to the sea trade port. It Also has an excellent restaurant.

He then went down to the Lobby bar and got himself his favorite Bourbon Manhattan on the rocks. While sipping his drink he contemplated on how he would contact a small contingent of Ukrainian freedom fighters so he could join them. He decided he would stay a couple of days and rest up before embarking on his next move.

He now had built an appetite, so he moved on to the hotel restaurant for dinner. He ordered a salad with Quinoa, Kamchatka crab and citrus, and for his main course Duck fillet sous-vide with mashed apple and saffron. He ordered a split of Ukrainian red wine. For dessert he got a Napoleon classic with vanilla ice cream and a glass of Brandy. He then retired to is room for a good night's rest.

The following morning, he went straight to the fitness center for an hour workout, then took a shower, dressed and went to the buffet breakfast. He then left the hotel and walked the streets nearby to get a perspective of the people living under the threat of the Russian Army. He is amazed at the resolve to fight the threat to the end and went He decided to send a white Rose to Cynthia to let her know he was OK. He included a note that said," It's cold here, miss you and hope I can come   soon to see you." That afternoon he went to the cocktail lounge for his afternoon perfect Bourbon Manhattan on the rocks and engaged in some conversation with the female bar ten tender. She asked him where he was from and what he was doing in Ukraine. He responded that he was from the

US and was there to help in the fight against the Russians and was trying to meet up with a special group of freedom fighters.

She disappeared for five minutes while he was finishing his drink and returned with another and placed in from of him. She said, "This one is on the house." Five minutes later a young man approached him while he was still at the bar. " Hello sir, I understand you are looking for the small militia group?" Michael realized he had suddenly made contact. "Yes sir". " Be ready tomorrow morning at six AM and someone will pick you up in the front of the hotel and bring you to meet one of our captains." "OK" With that the young guy left and the bar tender smiled at Michael.

Michael left the lounge and went to a restaurant for dinner and then went to his room to pack his things to get ready for his early morning meeting. He suddenly had a feeling of anxiety which always manifests itself whenever he is going to anticipate a new experience.

Six AM Michael was standing outside the hotel with a pack, and a small Duffel bag of clothing, and his special clandestine metal case. Suddenly a military jeep pulled up with a female driver in military garb and said get in. Michael threw his bags into the jeep and hopped into the front seat next to the driver who promptly sped away.

The traveled south and met up with a small Ukrainian military convoy and Michael was transferred to one of the small troop carriers. On the carrier there are a mix of women and young men freedom fighters. The gave Michael a set of military pants and shirt with and told him to put them on so he would fit in as one of them. One of the Ukrainian fighters questioned Michael as to why he was there to help them, and he told them that he had some special talents that might be of help to them, but he would discuss it with one of their commanders.

Hours later the convoy reached the town of Voznesenski where a major Ukrainian offensive is taking place. Michael is surprised to find out that 58,000 women are serving in the armed forces and many of them are in this offensive. He realizes that they need all the help that can get.

Michael told one of the commanders that if he could position him in a strategic location that was elevated that he would be able to sniper and assassinate some of the Russian officers and this would help bring about confusion to the Russian troops.

One of the Ukrainian soldiers led Michael to a partially bombed out building that could still be accessed to the roof top. Michael and the Ukrainian both positioned themselves in a prone position on the edge with sniper rifles about ten feet apart. Michael spotted a Russian tank about 200 yards away. The tank commander is standing in the open hatch of the tank with a phone directing the column of tanks. Michael had him in his scope cross hair and fired two quick shots. The Russian dropped over the front of the tank and the column stopped. He then drew a bead on the ground troops walking along withe tank.

With his high-powered scope, he could make out an officer leading the ground troops and took aim and fired another shot and killed he officer. The troops confused started to run in all directions and Michel and his partner picked them off one by one.

Their position was now compromised so they quickly exited the building and just in time. One of the tanks sent a shot and hit the top of the building and leveled it some more. They ran among a barrage of bullets and back into a safe place. A contingent of Ukrainian Marines attacked the Russians and wiped out five tanks and about 1000-foot soldiers.

Michael spent the next month in similar combat situations and finally decided that he had done his part and would find another way to help the effort. He made his way back to the boarder and crossed into Poland. He proceeded to Warsaw and went straight to the airport to fly to Paris. At the airport he sent a white rose and a note to Cynthia that read " I will see you in a couple of days in Paris, meet me, I will tell you where when I get there. Miss you, Michael."

Michael then went to the cocktail lounge at the airport and got himself a Bourbon Manhattan on the rocks as he sat and waited to board his plane.

Chapter 5   Paris

A couple hours later Michael walked off the plane and took a taxi to the American Embassy. He reported to the station chief and gave them a firsthand view of the war in Ukraine and some of his escapades. He urged them to notify Washington to beef up the aid of strategic weapons to the Ukrainian forces.

Michael told them that he was going to take a week off and then would report back to them.

He then left the Embassy and caught a taxi to his favorite hotel "Lotti" on 7 Rue Castiglione. It has a club like atmosphere and have resisted the modernization that many other hotels have undergone. It is an intimate version of a grand hotel, with spacious rooms and great amenities. It also has a great cocktail lounge.

When he got settled in and put his cloths in the closet and his small metal case in the safe. He took out his cell phone and called Cynthia. He told him where he was and that he could meet her the following day if she was free. She immediately responded and called back. "Michael happy to hear your voice, I missed you. Where can I meet you tomorrow and what time?" " Meet me at the Cafe De Flore at Five PM. It is a famous hangout of artists and intellectuals. It has a great atmosphere, and we will have our traditional cocktail. I also made a reservation for dinner at Laper'rouise." "Great Michael good choices, I am looking forward to seeing you."

Michael left the hotel and walked the adjacent streets and visited some of the little shops nearby. He decided to stop in and get some cheese, a ham sandwich, a cup of coffee and some French pastries.

He then strolled down the street and enjoyed the evening sun set falling over the majestic buildings of Paris. The city was coming alive with people out for the evening.

He returned to his hotel and decided to get a nightcap at the bar. He ordered a glass French Cognac drank it, and then went to his room for a much-needed good night's sleep.

The next morning Michael got up, put on his sweats and sneakers, and left the hotel for a two-mile run. He then returned and took a dip in the pool, went for breakfast of French croissant, pastries, and coffee. He then decided to take a walk on the left bank along the river to take in the sights.

Michael stopped into the shop Marionnaud and purchased a small bottle of Cynthia's expensive favorite Perfume. He had it wrapped in gold paper with a red ribbon and bow around the small box and placed it in his pocket. He then strolled the streets and shops and bought himself a pair of Black boots. He stopped at a men's shop and purchased a pair pf Jeans. He spent the rest of the day sitting on the balcony with his laptop sipping a cup of coffee and searching for background information on Russian Oligarchs that have escaped from view with their yachts. He homed in on a guy that is pro ported to be a special associate of the Russian President. He was of special interest to him because the guy was supposed to be a former member of the KGB and became wealthy on the backs of innocent Russians. His Yacht was last seen anchored in the Bay of Biscay off the Ilie d' Oleron opposite the city of La Rochelle on the French coast. Michael decided that this would be his next target.

He left the balcony and went back into his bedroom, put his laptop away, took a shower and dressed for dinner. He put on a pair of designer jeans, a grey turtleneck, his new boots, and his black leather jacket. He put his small gift in his pocket and called a taxi to take him to the Cafe De Flores. It was a balmy evening in Paris, and he arrived at 4:45 PM and sat down at a table outside the cafe waiting for Cynthia to arrive. He ordered two drinks knowing that she would show up within a few minutes.

At 5:03 PM Cynthia's black car pulled up, she got out and saw Michael sitting at a table. She walked briskly to him, and he stood up. She grabbed him and gave him a big hug and Kiss and said "I missed you, Michael. I was afraid something had happened to you" " I missed you too Cyn." With that they sat down, and the waiter brought their drinks to the table. Michael placed his little gold box in front of her as she sipped on her Vodka Martini and he on his Bourbon Manhattan on the Rocks.

She opened the little box and said " How sweet of you Michael, you remembered my favorite perfume. Thank you." She was a little disappointed that it was not a ring, but she knew he was not ready to give up his Clandestine world. They spent the next hour catching up on each other's past six months. They both left the cafe and Cynthia's driver took them to the restaurant.

They pulled up to Lape'rouse at about Six Thirty and entered the restaurant. For more than two centuries' guests and "cocottes" have flocked to the intimate and discrete ambiance of the restaurant.

Its walls ooze of French sensuality and Proustian heritage. They were escorted to one of the "Salons room La Reilf Otero which is a small private dining room with only one table. The entire restaurant is decorated with Fresco painted walls, chandeliers, and dark woodwork. It was the first Restaurant to be awarded three Michelin stars back in 1933 and was considered the house of pleasures since 1766. As they entered the room it is dimly lit by the chandelier hanging above the table and the single table for two is set with a red tablecloth. A candle center piece and elegant table setting for two.

Cynthia turned to Michael and said "This is fantastic Michael, I am impressed. I have never been here, but I have heard of it."

The waiter arrived and was dressed in a formal black suit white shirt with two menus a Wine menu and a white towel draped over his arm. "Mademoiselle e' Masseur can I get you a drink before dinner" Cynthia responded, " Yes sir I would like a Kir Royal " Michael said "That sounds good I will have one also. and bring us an order of La Charlotte de Pommes de Terre Noirmoutier, caviar and an order of Duck foie gras, corn & curry chutney, brioche."

After the waiter returned with their drinks and appetizers they sat and chatted while enjoying the ambiance of the room and their drinks. They then looked over the menu and discussed what they would order for dinner. They both homed in on one the Grand Classic of the house. Wellington

Beef for two with seasonal vegetables, with cocotte green herbs. It was served to Winston Churchill in 1940. The wine steward came to the table and gave Michael the wine book and said Can I get you some win sir" Michael handed it to Cynthia and said "Cyn you pick out one of the best wines from your Family Vineyard. She looked over the choices and said to the Waiter " Bring us a bottle of Louis Jadot 2000 Musigny Grand Cru and bring it now to let it breathe." "Yes Mademoiselle"

Michael and Cynthia chatted awhile, sipping their Kir' The bottle of wine was delivered immediately with an ornate decanter. The waiter gave Cynthia a taste of the wine and handed her the cork, which she sniffed and nodded approval. He then poured the bottle of wine into the decanter to breathe. The dinner lasted about 3 hours and the ordered Rose Baba Royal with Raspberries and homemade whipped cream and a sniffer of French Cognac.

After a three-hour dinner, Cynthia called her driver on the phone and told him they were ready to be picked up. They walked out the restaurant and almost immediately Cynthia's black Limo pulled, and the driver opened the door to the back seat.

Cynthia told her driver to take them to Michael's hotel and that she would call him when she was ready to be picked up. As they entered his room there was a bottle of Champaign and a box of chocolate covered strawberries on the cocktail table. Michael had arranged for it in anticipation of their rendezvous.

Michael opened the drape to his balcony and turned on some soothing music. They sat on his couch and had small talk and she asked him if he thought of retiring from his currant line of work. He responded that he did but it is still not time. She knew the answer ahead of time but had hoped for a different response. After a while they and a couple glades of Champaign the left the couch and entered Michael's bedroom. There they had a torrid sexual encounter that lasted into the wee hours of the morning.

Michael fell asleep and when he awoke Cynthia was gone. There was a note on his night table from Cynthia''' Thank you for a great evening, I am on my way to the family vineyard for a special event, wish you could be with me Cyn." Michael got up and rubbed his eyes and felt empty. He knows that he may not see her again for a great while if at all.

He dressed and went down for breakfast in the hotel restaurant. He spent the next two days taking in some sights of Paris. He then caught a taxi to the American Embassy and went straight to the section chief's office and informed him that he was going to pursue a Russian Oligarchy and his yacht. The station chief approved his mission and Michael left the Embassy.

Michael left the embassy and returned to his hotel, where he packed his things and called a taxi to take him to the train station. Here he caught a high-speed train from Paris to La Rochell. He had purchased a first-class ticket that gave him some special perks like access to the special bar lounge with free food and drinks, plusher seats, at seat meal service or access to the special dining car, and more.

Chapter 6   La Rochell France

The trip will take approximately 3 hours, so he decided to go to the bar lunge and get himself his perfect Bourbon Manhattan on the rocks. While enjoying his drink a good-looking blonde walked in and sat down next to him on an empty stool. She smiled at him, and Michael could not resist and struck up a conversation. "Hi, my name is Michael, are to going to La Rochell?" She spoke with a German English accent and responded, " I am Elka, and I am going there on Business" "Me too" What business are you in?" I Represent a German president of a large Food chain in Europe. I am here to seek out a Naval architect and designer. My boss wants to have a yacht built and in La Rochell are some of the bests. Why are you going there?" " Oh, I am going there on a holiday."

She handed him a card with a phone number and told him to call her and maybe they could get together for a drink. Michael took the card and decided he might just do that. He finished his drink, left the bar, and returned to his seat.

While at his seat he ordered a meal to be delivered at his seat with a carafe of French wine. As he dinned, he enjoyed the passing beautiful French countryside as they passed the quaint villages and farms.

Three hours later he left the train and walked through the train station and to a taxi stand. He took a taxi to the Hotel de Toiras. He then booked a room with a view of he harbors and Marina. His room had a direct view of all the large yachts anchored in the Harbor. He unpacked his clothes and put the contents of his clandestine metal case in the hotel room safe and put the case under the bed. He then went to the hotel bar and got himself his favorite drink, a perfect Bourbon Manhattan on the rocks and some crackers and cheese. It was a small bar with four blue padded bars but well stocked and a pleasant bar tender.

An hour later he returned to his room and went to his safe and pulled his pair of binoculars. He then went out on his little patio and peered through them at the various boats in the harbor. He homed in a large yacht at the end of the dock with a name of Amore Vero. owned by a Russian billionaire and one of Russian president's favorite people. He is a president of a large Russian company.

The yacht was scheduled to leave port within 48 hours after repairs. It had a crew of Russian and Ukrainians, but the French authorities have delayed its ability to leave preparing to seize the ship. Michael decides that he had to act fast. That night at about one AM in the morning he put on his black sweat suit and face mask and with his silencer and a grappling rope sneaked out of the hotel and walked quietly and carefully down the long concrete dock to the yacht. He noticed that there was a guard at the entrance of the yacht, but there was a smaller boat docked to the right of the yacht. The smaller boat was covered with a tarp, so he knew there was no one on it. That side of the yacht was dark, and the small boat was a perfect place for him to hide and wait for the right moment to try and board the yacht.

in about fifteen minutes later he saw a crewman walk by and enter a stairway and walk down to the main deck. Michael saw his opportunity and threw his gapling hook and caught the railing of the yacht. He shimmed up to the side and climbed over the railing and dropped to the floor. No had detected him so he entered the door to the cabin and made his way to what was the master bedroom.

The Oligarch was sound asleep, so Michael tiptoed over to his bed and put his silence on the side of his head and pulled the trigger twice. He then left the bedroom and walked out the door and down the rope to the small boat and then onto the dock.

He quietly returned to his hotel room. The following morning the news had reported the murder and the French authorities suspected that one of the Ukrainian crewmen might have taken revenge because of the War in Ukraine. Michael new he was in the clear and the French would be barking up the wrong tree.

He laid low for a day and then decided to call the Elka. He called her and asked her if she could meet him for a cocktail and dinner. She said yes and he told her to meet him at a restaurant called Les Flots on 1 Rue de la Chaine, La Rochelle at five thirty. She said OK and Michael called the Restaurant and made a reservation He asked for a table for two with a view of the port and they accommodated him.

At precisely Five forty-nine Elka walked in the door and spotted Michael sitting at the bar. Michael saw her dressed in a short shiny silver top. He said to himself (What a great metallic dress with a low cut at pair of legs) She said Hi Michael I am glad you called me for tonight, my business here finished up today and I will be leaving for Germany tomorrow. She sat down on the bar stool and her dress rose halfway up the legs and exposed her great legs. (Michael thought Wow!) He had already ordered himself his perfect Bourbon Manhattan on the rocks and was sipping it. As she sat down Michael said, "what would you like to drink/" She responded I think I will have a Savoy affair. Michael motioned to the bar tender and ordered the drink for Elka.

"Elka how did your business visit go?" Fine, I accomplished my goal and hired a Marine designer and architect, and they will be sending me their plans of a yacht for my boss to review."

" How has you holiday going?" "OK but I think I will be leaving tomorrow also; I am anxious to get back to work. Oh, I guess we should move over to our table." They were escorted by the Maître de a table with a great view of the harbor. " Said this a great table Michael what a spectacular view as the sun sets over the Harbor and Marina." "I agree"

You know that this Restaurant is one of the oldest in the city and recommended by Michelin. I was lucky to get a reservation because it is constantly booked solid." "It is great Michael I am looking forward to dinner." The waiter arrived at the table to take their order for dinner. For appetizers Michael ordered the producer's oyster plate (9 raw Oysters on a half shell. Elka ordered Langoustines and lemon Mayonnaise. For the main dish Michael ordered a pressed Veal shank Confit with spices, fine semolina and eggplant caviar with fresh herbs, blond grapes, and roasted almonds. She ordered Lobster strew and Beef shank with clear costume and season vegetables. Michael also ordered a bottle of 2003 Chevre Chamberton

They spent the next two hours chatting and enjoying the meal, the site, and the ambiance of the evening.

During their dessert of Souffles with Cognac and Liqueur cream, Elka invited Michael to have a night cap at her hotel. Michael hoped the evening would end with dinner and he said yes.

They left the Restaurant and caught a taxi to take them to Elka's hotel suite. They arrived and took the elevator to a room on the top floor overlooking the city. She went into the kitchenette and returned with two glasses and a half-gone bottle of Ansbach Cognac. She poured two glasses and she said "Prosit here's to a great evening." They clinked glasses and Michael took a sip of his drink.

Elka reached into her purse and pulled out another business card and handed it to Michael and said, " If you are ever in Garmisch Germany, maybe you can spend some time in my chalet." Michael realized that this was not only a visit invitation but that she was interested in starting a relationship. After about fifteen minutes she grabbed his hand and led him to the bedroom where she urged him to undress and dropped her dress and undergarments to the floor. Standing before him was the most majestic body he had ever seen. What ensued was a couple hours of passionate love making and they then both fell asleep. At about four in the morning while she was still sleeping Michael got, dressed, and left her a note, "See you in Garmisch Michael" He placed on the nightstand and left the room and hotel.

The following morning, he got up dressed, packed his things, and took a taxi to the train station. He then took a first-class high-speed train back to Paris. This time because he was so tired, he slept in the plush chair almost all the way back to Paris. He awoke just in time to see the train approach the city. He could see the Eiffel Tower in the distance. He gathered his things and waited as the train pulled into the station.

He caught a taxi to take him to his favorite hotel the Loti. He booked into a room with a balcony and then went to the lounge and bar and got himself a perfect Bourbon Manhattan on the rocks and relaxed for a while. He then went to the restaurant to get something to eat.

He relaxed for two days and the decided to go to the American Embassy and report to the section chief. When he met with the chief he was complimented on his latest accomplishment and that he was summoned to return to the US as soon as possible. He left the embassy and returned to his hotel. He packed his things and caught a taxi to the airport.

Michael caught a 2 PM flight from Paris Charles De Gaulle airport to Dulles nonstop. He booked La premiere first class and took advantage of all the perks. Plush seats that turned into a bed at night for sleeping, complete privacy curtain or retractable wall. He had a select check in and fast security check and with his diplomatic credentials was able bring his special silver clandestine case without search.

The flight takes Eight hours and 40 minutes, and he was served his favorite cocktail of Bourbon Manhattan on the rocks, and for dinner he had Lamb tenderloin, creamed and. vegetables. For dessert cheese selection, copped off with fresh fruit and sorbets. As well as a good French wine. Early in the morning he was serve freshly baked croissants and brioche pancakes, and fresh fruit. He got a freshly brewed cappuccino. He managed to get about 5 hours sleep and at 4 PM DC time his plane landed at Dulles airport.

Chapter 7   Washington DC

He was met at the baggage claim area by a man in a
black suit with a sign that read Mr. Vincent. Michael
approached him with his baggage and said, "Hi I'm
Him" The guy helped him with his bags and said,
"Follow me" He led him to a black SUV Parked in a
VIP parking area. Michael sat in the backseat and the
guy was driving him was silent and Michael said, "We
are we going?" " The guy responded "Langley"
Michael relaxed and collected his thoughts because he
would certainly be debriefed.

   The Black sedan pulled up to the entrance of CIA
headquarters and the guy said, "I will be waiting for
you when you finish your meeting, and you can leave
your luggage with me." Michael took his laptop and
slung it over shoulder and entered the building. He
walked past the wall of honor and passed to see if
there were any more stars on the wall. There were
some more, and he went over to the book to check
some of the names who had died in service. He was

surprised to see the name of another old partner. Once again, he wondered if he would ever escape such a fate.

He walked through security and took the elevator to the seventh floor. He entered the conference room after being checked by a secretary. About ten minutes later the door of the room opened and in walked Joe Cicciano, Rossard and the director of clandestine operations.

Michael stood up and shook their hands and they all greeted him with a smile. For the next hour they questioned him, and he did a core dump of information and the specifics of his mission. At the end of the meeting, they told him that he should take a week off and relax and that they have another Mission for him. With that the director produced a manila envelope and threw it on the table. and said "Here are all of the particulars of your next mission. Study it and a week from now leave town for your mission.

Michael took the envelope and put it in his laptop case, stood up and left the room. He couldn't wait to see what he was now going to encounter. He left the building, and the driver was waiting for him. He got in the SUV and told the driver to take him to Canopy hotel by Hilton on DC Wharf.

The hotel overlooked the Potomac River. It is walking distance to Arena stage and a mile from the National Mall. It is also in proximity to other Washington monuments and sites.

He checked into a room with a site of the Potomac and with a balcony with the view. He put all his clothes away and his valuables in the hotel safe and then put on his sweats and went down to the fitness center for a one-hour work out. He then took a dip in the hotel pool and swam for another half hour. He returned to his room and took a quick shower and dressed for dinner.

He made his way to the elevator and took it to Whiskey Charlie Rooftop bar. He sat down on one of the black plush leather bar stools and ordered a perfect Bourbon Manhattan on the rocks. The bar tender served his drink and placed a small glass bowl with nibbles and bites. The room was quiet and there were only a couple of people sitting at a small table in the lounge. He enjoyed the serenity and cherished his favorite cocktail for about forty-five minutes. Then his appetite kicked in, so he left the bar and took the elevator down to the Four Seasons Bourbon steak Restaurant.

Michael ordered a dozen oysters on a half shell, 12 oz Lamb chop from the Shenandoah valley, with sauteed Broccolini with garlic crumble and whipped mashed potatoes and fresh chives. He ordered a vintage bottle of Italian Amarone wine.

He polished off the whole bottle during dinner and was quite full and content, so he skipped dessert. He returned to his room and took out the envelope and sat down on his couch to read the contents. In the envelope there is a first-class airline ticket to Munich Germany, pictures of two individuals, and a Dossier on each of them. The first one is Abdul Aziz a Syrian known Isis fighter and the second is Eric Claus a native born eighteen-year-old German and an Isis recruit.

The two are among the sixteen known Jihadist hiding out in Munich. Abdul is the ringleader of the group and is the primary target. He is suspected to be in Northern Munich near where there is a Muslim Community and a Mosque.

For the next few days Michael did some site seeing in DC. He visited the Intelligence Museum, the ASA and CIA Museum. He Read the accounts of the Berlin Tunnel and the communications intelligence during the cold war. He was especially interested in these historical facts because his father was part of this history and was in the Army Security agency, stationed in Germany during the cold war.

Michael realized that he is following in his dad's foot steps to a degree. He finished his site sightseeing and returned to his hotel. He headed straight for the Charlie's Rooftop bar and had his afternoon perfect Bourbon Manhattan on the rocks. While enjoying his drink he contemplated what his father might have gone through in the service. He had a new sense of pride and wondered why his dad never talked about it.

He then moved on to the Bourbon Steak Four Seasons restaurant for dinner. For an appetizer he ordered Malossol Ostrea Caviar, and a 38 oz. Porterhouse steak with Bourbon steak sauce, a salt baked potato and wood grilled Cauliflower with Mala oil. He got a split of good Italian Barolo and a cup of cappuccino for dessert.

Following dinner, he returned to his room and relaxed and sat down to watch TV and study the contents of the envelope again and committed it to memory. At about Ten thirty PM he went to bed and set his alarm for six AM in the morning.

Michael got up and went to the fitness center for a one-hour workout. He then showered, dressed, and packed his things and put his bags near the door. He then went down to the hotel cafe and got himself a cup of coffee, a pastry and small bowl of fresh fruit. While eating breakfast he called a cab to pick him up in a half hour to take him to the airport.

Michael waited nervously in the front of the hotel with his bags and a taxi pulled up. He got in the cab with his bags and said, "Dulles airport please. "He caught a five thirty United flight, nonstop to Munich. The flight lasted eight hours and ten minutes and landed at seven AM in the morning. He traveled first class and was able to sleep most of the trip during the night.

Chapter 8   Munich Germany

When arriving at the main terminal he collected his bags and rented an Audi A5 Sport back car. He got one with a GPS and placed the address of the Pullman hotel in North Munich. It was a 25-minute drive from the airport and only seven minutes from Downtown. He booked a Superior room with a balcony that overlooked the city.

He unpacked his things and again stored his special Spy case in a safe place. He emptied the contents of it and placed whatever he could in the room safe. He then went down to the front desk where a pretty redhead was manning the desk and he asked her if she had a good points of interest map of Munich. She then reached down behind the desk and produced a couple of city maps. He said "Thanks Ms." He then returned to his room and pulled out his laptop and took it and the maps to his balcony.

He sat in one of the provided nice chairs and searched his laptop for Mosques in North Munich. He found the Masjid Mosque in the Islamic center located in the North Freiman section of Munich. It was the perfect place that the Jihadist would go to congregate and worship. He decided that this would be his stakeout location for the next couple of days. He decided that he would start the surveillance the following day.

He then left the hotel and went to the Munich Hofbräuhaus for some Bavarian beer and lunch. He ordered one of those big HB steins of fresh Bavarian beer and a Pork shank with gravy and a potato dumpling. He sat an enjoyed his lunch and listened to the Bavaria band play some om-papa music. He marveled at how the buxom waitress dressed in typical Bavarian cloths, could carry five of the steins filled with beer at the same time. He enjoyed seeing the various groups in various Bavarian garb enjoying the food and drink. He left the Hofbräuhaus and returned to the hotel.

When he arrived at the hotel he decided to go out. a swim in the pool and do a twenty-minute workout. He then went to the sauna and got himself a good sweat followed by a shower in his room. He then dressed and went down to Theos Bar for his evening cocktail.

He entered the Bar and sat at one of the cream-colored plush bar stools and ordered his perfect Bourbon on the Rocks.

He noticed a very good-looking women sitting at the end of the bar and his instinct kicked in. He was tempted to engage with her, but he then thought better of it because he did not want to jeopardize his mission. He had to stay focused. He finished his drink and left went to the Theos restaurant' for dinner.

He sat down at s the small tables in the back of the room and spent about ten minutes exploring the menu.   He decided on goat cheese with honey and lavender for an appetizer, and a Porterhouse steak with herb butter, Bearnaise creamy Pepper sauce and grilled vegetables. He ordered a split of Amarone Bertani Della Valpolicella Doc. For dessert he selected Sorbet of green apple and wild berries, and a glass of Spaetleser Weisswein. After dinner he returned to his room to watch TV and relax.

The following morning, he took a shower, dressed, and went down for breakfast. He had a hearty one because he knew it would be a long day without food.

He returned to his room and took out some of his disguise paraphernalia, hat, mustache, special glasses, and directional pen microphone and placed them in the pockets of his leather jacket.

He left the hotel, and he got is car and drove to the Mosque and Islamic community center. As he drove down the street he stopped and put on his disguise. He then proceeded to the Northern end of Munich and parked his car across the street opposite the entrance of the Mosque. He pulled out his binoculars and waited for people to come and go for prayer service. He also noticed on the large lawn outside the Mosque there was a large white tent where prayer service was taking place. There seem to be a lot of young men at the service in the tent. He homed in on the individuals in the tent.

When the service ended and the people started to exit the tent, Michael spotted his target walking out of the tent and to the community center building which among other things had small type rental rooms and apartments. It was the perfect place for his target to hide out. He now knew his instinct and research had paid off. Now how to get to his target and pull off his mission. He also noticed that there is a restaurant called Shandiz nearby and that maybe Abdul would go to eat.

Michael decided that he would check out the restaurant and eat there That evening. He walked in and was surprised to see the ambiance and beautiful table settings. He sat down at a small table toward the back of the room so he could observe other customers that came in and go. He ordered Sheep cheese with walnuts and olive, Kabab Tekka (a skewer of Lamb meat marinated in a garlic yogurt sauce and grilled), with a side dish of saffron basmati rice. He ordered a split of Brunello di Montalcino Il Valentino, and for dessert he had Pedrsion dates filled with walnuts served with black tea and he got a glass of Spätlese, Thomas Rath Liblich white wine.

He went for an early dinner so he could take his time and spend more time eating and observing. It paid off because about halfway through his meal he observed his target and the other the individual came into the restaurant and sit down at a table on far from his. He immediately took out his small directional recorder and took pictures with his glasses.

They were speaking Arabic to each other, and Michael could understand everything they said. They were talking in code, but he discerned that they were planning an attack somewhere and he decided that he had to act that night. He finished his meal and left the restaurant and waited across the street. About a half hour the two guys emerged from the restaurant and started to walk toward the Islam center.

Michael followed them and, in a few blocks, they reached a dark street and Michael accelerated his approach. They suddenly realized he was coming at them, and they turned around, but they were too slow, and Michael hit both with a Karate kick and knocked them down. With lightning speed, he pulled out his boot knife and cut their throats. He then ran back to his hotel and went straight to the bar for a double perfect Manhattan on the rocks.

The following day at eight thirty AM he packed his things, ate a quick breakfast and then fetched his car. He traveled south on Rt A95 for his trip to Garmisch. It's a One-hour trip but he decided to stop at the town of Wolfthtshausen for Lunch. He stopped his car at a Guest House named Humlbrau. When he walked in, he was met by young attractive blonde woman with her hair up in braids. She was dressed in a typical Bavarian dress. White Blouse, a black skirt with green embroidery design on the skirt and wide straps that flowed over her shoulders.

With a menu in hand, she greeted him with "Willcommen in Humplbrau sir, folgensie mir" Michael responded with "Tonka" and followed her to a table the window. He sat down and could see the beautiful snowcapped Bavarian mountains from the window. He ordered a Weiner schnitzel with zalzkailtoffen and a stein full of Bavarian beer. He spent about forty-five minutes eating lunch, enjoying the view of the mountains and the attractive waitress.

Chapter 9 Garmisch-Partenkirchen

He then left and proceeded on his way to Garmisch. About an hour later he arrived in Garmisch-Partenkirchen. As he drove into the center of town, he passed beautiful Bavarian buildings on the right and left of the street built with the traditional Bavarian style stucco, brick and wooden accents. On could see the snowcapped mountain up close, peeked by the famous Zukspitz. He stopped and parked his car in front of one of the beautiful gift shops. He pulled out the card with Elka's card and called her on his cell phone.

She answered "Hallo wer rufft an?" (Who is calling?) "It's me Michael I am in Garmisch and would like to see you" She responded in English "Great Michael I would be happy to see you again. Don't go to any hotel. You can stay at my Chalet. I have plenty of room and I am on the foothills of the mountains and between them and the city. She gave him directions from the town and her house.

As he hung up it started to snow and the rooftops, streets and cars started to get dusty. He knew that he best hurry to Elka's or he may not get through. It took him about fifteen minutes, and he pulled up to a beautiful A frame chalet, now covered with snow. She walked out to meet him dressed in slacks, boots, and a white wool sweater. She gave him a hug and helped him in with his bags.

They walked into the house through a small foyer that had four pairs of skis on a wood paneled wall and shelves with ski boots as well as ski jackets and pants hanging from hooks on the wall. That led to a small hallway that opened to a great room with stone and wood walls and ceilings. There is a stone fireplace with a plush white couch and chairs to match all places facing the fireplace. At the end of the great room there is an eight-bar stocked with all kinds of booze, including a wire rack to the left of the wall. To the right there is a shelf with about four trophies for skiing,

There is an open wooden arch leading to the kitchen that also has a fireplace open to it from the great room. It too is appointed with beautiful stone and wood accents throughout. Michael is impressed with the ambiance of each room. Elka continued to give him a tour of the house, the Master suite, her den, and the guestroom. She then said, "Follow me Michael" She led him up a wooden stair up to the loft. There is a small sofa and plush chair, a telescope pointed out of a large glass window toward the Mountains.

Michael thought (Wow what a spectacular view) "Michael do you ski?" "I have a few times back in the States, but I haven't for years." "Look through the scope, do you see that little house on the side of the Mountain peak?" "Yes" "Tomorrow, I will take you there for Lunch. Only we have walk there on skies. It will be worth it because when we get there you will meet a nice family, Ludwig and his wife Hannah and their ten-year-old girl Loreiel. They will serve you a great lunch and the Husband will play a guitar; Angelica will sing, and they will entertain you.

They left the loft and returned to the great room. Elka started a fire in the fireplace, and they sat down on the plush couch and watched the snow falling out the window. The room was nice, cozy and Michael was content and comfortable. "Michael, can I make you a drink? I will make dinner and you can enjoy the fire while prepare it." "Yes Elka, do you have Bourbon and vermouth?" "Yes, I do" "Well I will have a Bourbon Manhattan on the rocks, made with half sweet and a half dry vermouth, if you have bitters add a dash." "OK you got it." She returned to the kitchen and in a few minutes returned with his drink and said "Prost I will be back soon.

A couple of minutes later she returned with a small tray of Obazat spread on small pieces of rustic bread, (A cheese like spread made in Germany) "This will tide you over while finish preparing dinner." in about eight minutes she returned with a glass of white wine and sat down on the couch next to Michael. "Dinner is in the oven and will be ready in about twenty minutes" They both sat there and chatted for a while and enjoyed the glow of the fire and the falling snow.

Twenty minutes later he said let's go, it's time for dinner and she led him into the kitchen. The round table was set with a red tablecloth and a candle in the center. A bottle of 2005 Hans Wirsching Franconian wine was open and breathing. Two typical Bavarian wine glasses with a wide green stem were set along with two place setting.

Michael sat down and Elka went to the oven and pulled out a metal pan stuffed Duck with tart apples. She then took a dish of Knodel (potato dumpling) and another dish of red cabbage and placed them on the table. She then proceeded to serve portions to both their plates and said, "Help yourself to more when you finish what I gave you".

Michael thought (What a multi-talented woman.) The meal was great and prepared to perfection. He really enjoyed the Duck especially and the Franconian wine for dessert she served a homemade apple strudel and coffee, and a small glass of Ansbach. Following dinner, they moved to the great room on the plush couch opposite the glowing fireplace. They chatted for about one hour and a half and exchanged their backgrounds. Michael was careful not to mention his association with the US government. As the fire dwindled to just embers, she took his hand and said "We best go to bed soon, but first we can take steam bath in my sauna. She led him to the guest bedroom, opened the closet and pulled out a terry cloth bathrobe and slippers and threw them on the bed "Here Michael put these on, and I will be back in a couple of minutes.

She returned in ten Minuets dressed in a bathrobe and said, "Come on Michael." She led him to her master bedroom that is a doorway just inside her room. He opened it and it was a cedar walled small sauna with a bench and it was already starting to steam up the room. She then took off the robe and hung it up on a hook, exposing her beautiful statuesque naked body. She told Michael to do the same and he did.

The experience was invigorating and sensual. It urged his body of all the toxin in it. After a half hour she said" Now we will take a cold shower" and she led him to her walk-in shower and turned the water on. She got in and coxed Michael to do the same This is the first time he would take a shower with a naked woman. It looked like a wonderful experience.

After the shower She took his hand and walked him over to her bed. She pushed him down and straddled him Kissed him and proceeded to make enthusiastic love to him for forty-five minutes. She then smiled and said, "We both best get some sleep because tomorrow will be a big Physical day," Michael retired to the guest room, took a quick warm shower, and went to bed.

At Seven AM Elka woke him up out a sound sleep and said "Michael in that dresser there is a pair of Long Underwear, and a white wool sweater. You will need them for the cold, and in the closet, there are a couple pairs of ski pants, I am sure one will fit you because they were bought for my boss who visits me occasionally to go skiing and he is about your height. When you're finished come to the kitchen.

Michael walked into the kitchen dressed in a pair of red ski pants and the white sweater. The table was set for breakfast. There were two glasses of orange juice, a platter of assorted hams Liverwurst and sausages, including wild Bratwurst, a plate of assorted cheese, a soft bold egg for each of them and a basket of breads including the typical Bavarian large pretzel. There is an assortment of small dishes of sweat mustard, and jams. He sat down and said "Wow Elka what a spread." "You will need the energy for your walk up the Mountain. Would you like a cup of coffee with Breakfast or a beer? Some Bavarian drink beer with breakfast" "I will have coffee please". After a hardy breakfast, Erika said "Come on Michael, it's time to climb a mountain." She threw him a Black Parker with a hood and said put this on. They then got into her Mercedes and drove southeast on Rt 23. They rode through the long tunnel on the outskirts of Garmisch and into the countryside, passing little villages, farms, and an occasional house.

An Hour later they reached the Zugspitze Plaza and parked the car. They unloaded the skis and carried them to the base of the snow-covered Mountain. They put them on an Elka instructed Michael on how to walk up the hill on skies sideways, one step at a time. Their destination is the small house halfway up the Mountain. It took them an hour and forty-five minutes and Michael was glad to arrive at the cute chalet on Zugspitze Mountain. He we aching and hungry. They took off the skies and entered the house. Next to the house there is a small barn with two cows, a couple of pigs and chickens.

The husband Ludwig meets them, and he led them inside and to a table in the center of the room'. The room was adorned with unique Bavarian woodwork and stone and the woodwork was accented with a green scrolling design. Elka introduced Michael to the family, and they sat down. Ludwig went to a doorway to led to a shed and came back with two bottles of Dunkel beer and two glass steins. He placed them on the table in front of Elka and Michael and poured each bottle into the glass Steins. Hannah then served them a dish of Schweine Braten (Roast Pork) with Pampfnuden (dumpling) and red cabbage. For dessert they were served Bavarian cream with fresh fruit and a copper cup of Gluhwein. (Hot mulled wine.) During dinner they were entertained by Ludwig playing his guitar and his daughter singing Bavarian songs.

When dinner was over Elka thanked them and paid them for their hospitality. She explained to Michael that is the way they make a living by visitors to their home for a meal when skiing on the mountain. They left the house and fetched their skis that were leaning against the house outside the doorway. They put them on and Elka said "We are going to ski down the hill and you will do what they call a snowplow and go slow until you reach the bottom where there is a tow bar ski lift. Then we will spend the rest of the day skiing up and down this slope."

Michael had to learn how to grab the tow bar with one hand and grab the rope behind him to ascend the hill. After about three trips up and down the slope he felt brave and instead of snow plowing he straightened his skis and flew down the slope. When he reached the bottom, he could not stop and plowed into a snowbank to stop. As he picked himself out of the snow Elka laughed and said, "Let me teach you how to stop on your skis" She proceeded to do just that.

The sun was slowly starting to sink behind a mountain and shined a pink sky over the snow. They decided to stop for the day and returned to the car. Elka drove back north. During the trip back Michael said "Elka this has been great how about letting me take you out to dinner in Garmisch?" "OK Michael that would be nice."

On the way back Michael said "Let us stop at the Schloss Elmu hotel, it has the best restaurant in

Munich and one of the best in Germany, it has been awarded 2 Michelin stars. "That would be wonderful Michael." About a half hour they pulled up the hotel, parked the car and entered the Luce D' Oro restaurant. They were seated at a secluded table in the back of the room which was dimly lit with starburst lights on the dark wooden walls and dimly lit ceiling lights throughout. candle in the center and napkins in a silver napkin holder, wine glasses and silver ware place setting for two.

They took a few minutes reviewing the menu and then the waiter approached their table and asked if he could get them something to drink. Mounted on the dark wooden walls are starburst lights and there are ceiling lights dimly lit. The table is set with a white linen cloth and for two with a lighted candle in the center of the table, a silver napkin holder with a white linen napkin, silver place settings and wine glasses.

Michael ordered a bottle of Brut Champaign and they both decided to go with the chef's special six course tasting dinner paired with various wines. It started with Icelandic Norway Lobster, followed by Quail Breast and Jerusalem artichokes cooked in broth and grated truffles, served with a glass of Sauvignon Blanc, Grand Fume, Fournier Pere et fils, Loire valley. Then Squid stuffed with rice and black Truffle candied in olive oil. The next course is Rack of Limousin veal with sweetbreads and Romaine salad. Served with a glass of Concreto Malbec from south America. This was followed by Duck Foe Gras and braised duck legs in reduced red wine with Lentils and young sprouts. Served with a glass of Chabertine. The meal is topped off with a dessert5t of Pears in Cassis, served with a Glass of Riesling

 Kabinett, Sclossgut Diel, Nahe Germany.

Michael picked up the tab and said "Elka thank you for great day" "Michael thank you; I enjoyed every minute of it, and dinner was one I will remember for a long time." They left the restaurant and proceeded to Elka's house. Michael spent that night and another there and they had to leave. Elka helped him take his bags and put them in his car. She waved goodbye and threw him a kiss as he pulled away. He drove straight to the Munich airport, turned in his car and caught a flight straight from Munich to Washington DC.

Chapter 10   Back in the USA

He had not notified anyone he was returning so he was on his own to get transportation once he arrived in Washington. He pondered on whether he should report in or quit the game. He decided to take a few days off and visit his parents in Florida. He flew into Jacksonville airport, rented a cart, and drove to Central Florida to his parents' house in Palm Coast. He did not inform them ahead of time but drove up to their driveway, parked the car and rang their bell. His Father answered the door and was surprised to see his son standing there. He hugged his son and called Michael's mother who was in the kitchen preparing dinner. She put her cooking utensil down and responded to go to the front door. She was surprised and happy to see their son and gave him a big hug. Michel's father helped in with his luggage and brought them to the guest room that had still contained Michael's memorabilia (trophies awards, medals etc.)

Michael's mom returned to her cooking and set an extra dish at the table for Michael. His dad asked him if he would like cocktail, and Michael said, "Yes Dad if you have my favorite." "Of course, Michael, coming right up Your mother and I will join you, but we will our Vodka Martini on the rocks. Dinner was one of Michael and his favorite Spiedini (stuffed rolled veal with cheese, tomato paste, and breadcrumbs) on a skewer with bay leaves and onion, dipped in olive oil and breadcrumbs and then broiled. She made a big salad and some garlic bread. Michael's dad brought a bottle of Sicilian red wine, opened It, and let it breath.

Michael was in seventh heaven and realized how he missed his parents and is mom's cooking and his dad's love for good wine. He realized that they both brought him up to enjoy the good things, in life, an education as well as a patriotic spirit. Having a renewed respect for both he asked them a million questions at dinner about their past, history and family heritage. After dinner the sat on their lanai and chatted until sunset. They then all retired for the evening and Michael slept in the new bed in the guest room.

The next day Michael's Mom and Dad had an appointment with a doctor for a checkup. While Michael waited for them to return, he went into his dad's office which is a third bedroom converted to his office with a Murphy bed, bookshelves, desk and is dad's computer. He noticed a binder that was marked ASA. He pulled off the shelf, sat down at the desk and looked through it. He was amazed at the role his dad played during the cold war and that he had arrived in Germany during the last days of the occupation. He saw pictures of German individuals and his lifelong buddy who now lives in Nebraska.

He looked over the numerous books on the shelves that contained some of his father's old textbooks, and biographies of famous people. One book that caught his eye was a textbook of constitutional studies. While he was perusing through it his parents returned.

Knowing that both his parents were getting old and that they both had health issues, he was concerned. He said, "How did go folks?" "Fine son, were doing OK." Michael spent the next few days in the comfort of his family and then decided it was time to return to Washington. He packed up is things loaded them in the car drove back to Washington DC. It was a long drive, so he stopped off at

Gettysburg slept overnight and then took in the site of the great civil war battle and then went on to DC. He drove to Tyson VA. And checked into the Watermark Hotel only 3.2 miles from CIA HQ in an upscale community on the west side of the city. He booked a one-bedroom terrace suite, which overlooked the city. The suite has a full kitchen with a small refrigerator and microwave. It has a living room, with a couch, TV, and an ergonomic desk, In room safe. The bedroom has luxury bedding and towels I the bath which has a walk in Glass shower.

He settled in and then went to the fitness center that is equipped with 14 pieces of various aerobic equipment. for a one-hour workout. He then took a shower, dressed, and headed for the Wren and sat down at the hotel bar for his afternoon cocktail. He ordered his favorite perfect Bourbon Manhattan and sat their people watching in a terribly busy atmosphere. He decided to eat dinner sitting at the bar. he ordered a dozen raw oysters with white wine Mignonette cocktail sauce, roasted baby beets with Mascarpone cheese, baby arugula and pistachio vinaigrette. For the main dish he ordered Jukusei Kamo (Aged duck breast with sweet Miso eggplant and Duck liver mousse He ordered a bottle of cold Saki with a glass of ice and a slice of Lime.

When he finished dinner, he retired to his room to watch TV and get a god night's sleep.

The following morning, he got up, put on his sweats and went down to the fitness center for a workout. He then took a shower dressed and went to breakfast at the Aviary restaurant and ate a healthy breakfast of juice, fresh fruit, yogurt, granola, and freshly baked goods from a local baker. While at breakfast he called HQ and let them know that he was in town and would be coming in at 10 AM that morning.

At nine forty-five he took his laptop, slung it over his shoulder and entered the elevator and took it to the lobby and called for a cab. It only took a few minutes and one pulled up. He got in and instructed the driver to take him to CIA HQ. Twenty minutes later they pulled up to the front entrance of the building.

He paid the driver and briskly walked into the building, passed the CIA logo in the marble floor and passed the wall of honor, flashed his badge to the guard and proceeded to the elevator. He took it to the top floor flashed it to the receptionist and walked down the hall to the conference room. He walked in at about 5 minutes to ten.

His handler, Joe Cicciano and Rossard were all sitting around the table and got up as Michael entered the room. They greeted him with congratulations on his successful mission. In the room on the conference table there is a projector. They asked Michael if he could share any pictures of his mission. He said yes and hooked up his laptop proceeded to show them pictures of his surveillance.

They were impressed and where he has been for the last two weeks. He spoke, "After my mission I went to Germany to visit the site of my Fathers old Intelligence Army base in Herzogenaurach. The American Military turned it over to the Adidas company, who now use as a meeting site for the company. They were kind enough to give me a tour of the site and some of the original buildings are still there.

After that I went to Garmisch for a couple of days of Skiing and R&R. Then I visited my folks in Florida for a couple of days. I hope you understand that if I am to continue to be effective, my movements and whereabouts can only be known by me. They all acknowledged it and shook their heads in approval. I am now ready for my next assignment gentlemen. With that Michael's handler got up and plugged in his laptop computer and started his presentation.

"This picture of a young man on his motorcycle is student of advanced international studies at John Hopkins. This course is usually reserved for high military or government dignitaries, he was able to get admittance to the course. He goes by the name of George Allen but, his name is Gregory Petrov a suspected Russian spy. He is well liked by the students, but they do not know him.

The next picture is a captain in the US army that likes to ride his bike with Gregory and is suspected to be part of the cell. His name is Ivan Chertoff and is suspected of being a Russian sympathizer and possibly part of the spy ring. There is a third individual. Here is his picture. H is a student at John Hopkins also. He has been seen meeting with the two others in cafes on road trips and in local bars. Gregory is suspected to be the leader of the group and he and the captain must be taken out. However, it must look like an accident."

"OK I understand. This may take me awhile it is not going to be easy." "We understand Michael, Good luck" "When and if I succeed, I want you all to know that I will be taking a year off and returning to Japan for a rejuvenation of my Samurai studies. "OK Michael, do you have plan?" "Yes, but I will let you know when it's over. Michael then left the meeting and returned to his hotel. He researched for an apartment close to the university that graduate students rent and he came up with the Maryland apartments only .1 mile from the school. The next day he called and asked for the availability of a one room, one bath apartment. There is one available that suits his needs. He took a cab to the location to check it out. He entered the rental office and asked for a tour of the apartment he wanted. He was satisfied and he booked it.

He returned to the hotel and packed his things. Then went to dinner at one of the local restaurants. After dinner he called a taxi to take him to the Maryland apartments where he moved into his new apartment. He got a good night's sleep and the following morning worked out in the fitness center at the apartments. He then walked down the street to a coffee shop and got a bagel and a cup of coffee.

Michael walked to the John Hopkins University and entered the registrar's office. He asked to see a catalog of courses for graduate students. Michael presented his academic credentials. The course he wanted, a course in International was going to start in one week so he enrolled. He then returned to his apartment and searched the newspaper for a motorcycle for sale. He found a 2016 Cherry red Harley Davidson for sale for $15,000. He called the owner and offered him $13,000. The owner said he would let it go for $13,800> Michael said "OK I will come and pick it up. Michael took a cab to the site of the owner and rang his doorbell. A guy in his late fifties answered the door and Michael said Hi I am to buy your bike. The guy said "Alright wait while I open the garage door" Michael then walked over to the garage and watched it open. The guy then rolled out the bike. Michael was pleased at its looks and said, "Can I start it up and see how it sounds?" "Sure" With that Michael straddled the bike and pumped the starter. It started immediately and sounded good, it was in good shape and was well taken care of.

The guy presented Michael with the registration and Michael gave him a certified check for the bike and said thank you. He then hopped on the bike, stared it and rode away. He immediately drove to a Motorcycle outfitting store and bought himself a full-face black helmet, a Tour master draft black jacket, and a pair of Leott Moto 1.5 grip gloves. His plan was slowly taking place. He then drove from the cycle outfitting store to is apartment.

The net order of business is now to find out where most of the students hang out off campus. He asked a young lady in the rental office where the students hang out and she told him about a place called PJ's pub in Charles Village. Michael decided to check it out.

He drove his bike there and parked it outside. He walked in and the place was jam packed with students drinking, eating, and having a ball. He said to himself this the place. They offered a pint of beer for only $3 on Thursday college night and $10 for a pitcher of beer on Sat. College football day. They also have simple inexpensive menu of Nachos, French fries, Pizza, Burgers, Quesadillas, and wraps. He decided to get a pint of beer, and a Burger with French fries.

He sat down at a table that was open and in no time felt he was asked by a couple of students if they could sit at his table. He said "sure and they did and ordered pints of beer. On of the guys said, "High I'm Jack, I haven't seen you here before are you a new?" "Michael responded "Yes my name's Michael and I just enrolled in the University today." (Michael thought (How perfect he could begin to be part of the social scene.

Jack asked Michael what he is enrolled in, and he told him. With jack was another guy by the name Bill who responded to Michael by saying "I know a guy in that Major his name is George. He will probably come on Sat. for game day". (Michael thought Bingo I now have a possible opportunity of meeting my target without suspicion.) Michael finished his beer and burger and left PJ's while the place was still jumping.

He got on his Bike and drove back to his apartment. He parked his bike in the garage in the space allotted to him. Locked it up and carried his helmet to the elevator and took it to the twelfth floor to his apartment.

Michael visited a local grocer, bought some groceries to stock his kitchen and went to a liqueur store to buy a bottle of Makers Mark Bourbon, Two bottles of Vermouth, some bitters, and Maraschino cherries. He was now stocked for the long hall. He immediately made himself a perfect Bourbon Manhattan on the rocks, threw off his boots, and sat down on his patio to relax. He sipped his drink and looked out on the city as the sun started to drop behind the buildings. When he finished his drink, he retired to his bedroom and went to sleep.

For the next two weeks Michael drove his bike to class, frequented the student union and PJ's, in the hopes that he would run into his target. On the second football Saturday he pulled up to PJ's and parked his bike outside. As he was entering the Pub, two motorcycles pulled up and parked next to his. It was George (Gregory) and his Lt. Buddy Ivan.

The said "Hi, Nice Bike" "Michael responded Hi Thanks." They all entered PJ's together and Michael went to a table where Jack and his friend was sitting. George and Ivan went to a different table. It was about one PM in the afternoon and the John Hopkins football game was about to begin. It was an away game, so PJs was packed with students drinking beer and watching various TVs throughout the pub.

Michael ordered a pint of beer and a personal small cheese pizza. While he was drinking his beer, Jack said "Hi nice to see you again, by the way the guy I told you about is here today, if you want, I can introduce you to him." "That would be nice, Thank you." Jack escorted Michael to the table where George and Ivan were sharing a pitcher of beer and eating Nachos. He introduced Michael to them, and they invited him to sit with them.

They asked Michael what he was studying at the University, and he told them. George said, "What a coincident I am in the same major." Ivan said. "We take bike trips in the countryside once in a while, are interested in Joining us?" Michael responded, "Yes if my schedule permits it." He did not want to be too obvious. They exchanged Emails so they could communicate with one another, and Ivan said "Here is my face book site. You can see some of the pictures we have taken on our trips." With that Michael finished his beer and said "Thanks guys I must go and study for an exam. See you around." Michael got up and left the Pub.

He was happy to make the important connection and went straight to his apartment. He wasted no time in checking out Ivan's website. He checked out all the pictures and comments of people who communicated with him. He went a step further and checked out both Ivan and George on LinkedIn, and George's face book page. He noted the pattern of photos and mutual contacts of both. There were several military contacts, and student contacts from other universities.

They both belong to a club called Global technology club. It is managed by George and has 107 members. The mission of the club stated is "The sharing of technology development worldwide to improve the life of people." The site asks for technology people to Join and members to provide information on emerging technological advancements. The red flag went up for Michael and he knew that it is a recruitment and intelligence information gathering tool for Russian spies.

Michael Joined the club with a fictitious name and a fictitious job title for a sensitive job with a small aeronautical company. He waited while he was approved for membership. Forty-eight hours later he was approved of the club and was able to read all the messages posted by the members. He also now had access to the membership list which he copied so he could research them.

He now had to devise a plan on how to eliminate George and Ivan. When he checked his Email, he got a message from George that they were going for a bike rod the next day in the VA countryside at 1:00 PM and asking him if he was interested in Joining them. If he was, they were going to meet at PJ's. Michael saw this as an opportunity and responded that he was interested and would meet them. The following day he pulled up to PJs at five minutes before one and he noticed that George and Ivan's bikes were already parked outside PJ's. He quickly laced two small explosive devices and a pint of Gin in their saddlebags and entered the pub. They were having a beer and he joined them for a glass of beer.

About 20 minutes later they all left mounted their bikes and headed out on their trip. As they approached rural part of Virginia with open fields, trees, and farmland. He noticed that it was void of people and no possible witnesses. He took his detonator out of his pocket and waited for the proper moment. They soon came to a high bridge over a ravine and Michael stopped and pressed the button on his device. Both bikes exploded and went out of control and plunged over the side of the bridge 1000 feet to the bottom of the ravine. Michael turned his bike around and drove it home.

When he got home, he made himself a perfect Manhattan on the rocks, flipped off his boots and sat down to watch the news. The evening news had a story about two men killed in an accident at the VA Bridge. Speculation in the news had it that they were drunk because of the smell of gin, but they could not tell for sure. Michael proceeded to compile a list of the club members and he e-mailed a note to his handler at CIA HQ. His note told them that all the people on the list should be subject to surveillance and that some of them may be spies and some just Russian sympathizer. He also gave his handler his access to the club so they could continue to monitor it. He ended his note by telling him that as he had promised, he was going to take a refreshment sabbatical and will be out of reach for six months.

Michael completed the course at the University so as not to bring suspicion on him. He then did not enroll in any other courses, and he informed his landlord that he would be vacating his apartment in two weeks. He placed an ad in the local newspaper to sell his motorcycle and sold it in six days for $15,000. shipped most of his clothes to his parents, packed a hiking pack with some essentials. Two days later at seven AM he took a cab to the airport and booked a flight to Japan. He booked a first-class seat on DL3733 which has a stopover in Detroit and then changed to flight 275 direct to Tokyo Japan. The flight from Detroit took 13 hours and five minutes.

During the flight to Japan, he took advantage of all the first-class amenities like 24-hour hot food service, snacks, Cocktails, TV, Wi-Fi etc. He also was able to get a few hours rest.

Chapter 11 JAPAN

When he arrived in Tokyo, he took a taxi to the JR
Shinjuku train station and a train on the Chud line
limited express Zusato to Kofus station. There he
took the train to Manobo station. From Manobo
station he took a taxi to Mino Busan rope way. From
there he walked to the Kuon-ji temple founded in
1281, in Yamanashi. The temple was the headquarters
if Nic Hiren, a branch of Buddhism established by the
priest Nic Hiren. After a short visit to the temple, he
took the "East Course" trail behind the temple to
climb the Manobo Mt.

He entered the enormous Senmon Gate, walked
through the cobblestone path to a steep 287 step
stone staircase, flanked by towering cedars. He then
climbed 720 meters. He then climbed the many stairs
and entered the unpaved trail and hiked through the
wild open forest trail.

In his pack he only carried his Gee, a small
complement of under ware, sandals. his knife, the
novel Masashi and the Book of Five rings. Having

visited the mountain before he is aware that the forest is filled with wild animals, (bears, deer, wild boar etc.) Along the way he passes numerous temples, statues and various objects related to Buddhism.

About ninety percent up the mountain, he came to the Waterfall, pouring down the mountain into a clear water lake. He then found the cave nearby where he spent the last time on the mountain. Along the way he passes bright crimson berries of the Nandina shrub. The bush is long believed to have the power to dispel evil and misfortune. Michael clipped a small branch with some berries and put it in his pack. It is now late fall, and the summit is surrounded by thick groves of Cedar, cypress, and maple with shades of gold and vermilion still blocking the sunlight keeping the path cool. The fresh mountain air and the color of autumn provides Michael with a sense of tranquility.

As Michael reached his desired highest point, he could see the sun rising over the tip of Mt. Fuji, Because the sun glimmers over its peak it Is called "diamond Fuji." He entered the cave and was surprised it was just as he had left it. He then took off his pack and placed Its contents on a stone shelf in the cave. He then stripped down to a pair of shorts and walked a few yards to the small clear lake and jumped in with his knife tucked in. He proceeded to take a refreshing swim and caught fish with his knife. He gathered some dry grass, twigs and a couple dry tree branches and returned to cave and built a fire.

He cooked the fish over the fire, ate it and then spread out his small blanket and went to sleep while the fire was reduced to embers. The following early morning he arose as the sun was tipping over the Mountain and he was to start a program of rigorous training. The following six months he would train eight hours each day without rest, by doing 150 squats, 150 push-ups, 150 jumps over a certain flax plant and stand under the buffeting cold waterfall naked for an hour. He would break stones with his hands. He would use trees as makiwara with repeating strikes. Each day he would spend time studying the two books he brought with him. Her lived on edible Mountain vegetables such as Butter bur buds, ostrich teen sprouts, wild Rocambole and Angelic buds all of which grow in the Mountains. He either would eat them raw or boil them and add them to the fish or meat that he would catch.

Each day in addition to his physical training he would practice his favorite Kata. When wading in the cool lake he would catch fish with his bare hands. He cut down a bamboo pole and fashioned it as a spear. One morning early he grabbed his spear and walked down to the lake and hid in a bush, suddenly a small wild boar wen t the water's edge drink and Michael threw his spear with great force and killed the boar. This provided him with some meat which he smoked and had available for a couple of months.

After six months of living in the wild on the mountain, he was rejuvenated in spirit, mind, and body. However, he was not satisfied and decided he wanted to expand his horizon by studying the art of Japanese sword fighting. He hiked down to the Mino Busan rope way station and took it down to the town of Manobo. The trip only took him about eight minutes. There he took a train back to Tokyo.

When Michael reached Tokyo, he got a room at the Hyatt Centric Ginza Tokyo hotel. He checked in to a Deluxe king room. It is a top-notch hotel with all the amenities you can think of.

He selected the hotel because it was in the Ginza district and close to where he plans to go to study swordsmanship. It also has a great bar, restaurant, and fitness center. After he settled into his room, he went down to the Nami Ike 667 Bar. It was situated in the restaurant and had about 19 leather bar stools and had a blue glass lighted ambiance. Michael decided to have a drink at the bar and ordered his long-awaited perfect Bourbon Manhattan the rocks. He finished his drink and then moved to a table to have dinner.

For an appetizer, Michael ordered Marinated Hokkaido Flounder with Tokyo vegetables and soy sauce, a cup of Lobster bisque with truffle and Oven roasted Akigawa Wagyu beef sirloin with Tokyo vegetables for the main course. He ordered a half bottle of Domain Phillipe Charlopin Marsannay Les E'cdhezots 2019, red wine. For dessert he got Cheesecake, with olive oil and salted sherbet and grapes.

Following dinner, he took a walk through the streets of Ginza which is crowded with tourists and residents, frequenting the many shops, restaurants and places of entertainment and then returned to his hotel for a good night's rest. The following morning, he had room service bring him breakfast and then took a shower and dressed. He left the hotel and walked to Hisui Tokyo in the Koizumi building at 5F Ginza 4-3-13 Chuo ward. This is the location of Hisui Tokyo studio of instruction for the Samurai way. The schools offer an authentic Batto course with comprehensive instruction in the art of swordsmanship with a live Katana. (Japanese sword). Taught by Master Suiju Kaito.

In addition, the school teaches Japanese calligraphy and the Tea Ceremony to round out the way of the Samurai. Michael signed up for a six-week program. First, he learned the technique of cutting at 45-degree angles, from either side. Then he learned to master a variety of cutting techniques such as horizontal cutting and a 5-form cut. He is taught the movements of the Samurai and Hyoho Niten Ichai-Ryu (2 sword fighting with a Katana and a Wakizaski). This is called "Two Heavens as one. In the time of the Samurai, he Wakizaski the shorter sword was used primly as defensive weapon while the Samurai used the Katana to strike.

After his six weeks of training in the way of the Samurai, he was given a certification to become a sword instructor. This now rounded out his martial arts skills.

He then packed his things and moved out of the hotel and called a taxi to take him to the airport. Here he caught a fight back to the United States.

CHAPTER 12   BACK IN THE USA

It was early in the morning and the 747 dropped down through the clouds and landed in Washington DC Dulles airport. Michael exited the plane and walked through the terminal to the baggage area. He picked up his Backpack thew his laptop case over his shoulder and caught a taxi outside the terminal. When he entered the cab, he instructed the driver to take him directly to CIA HQ.

He arrived at the building, played the driver for the fair grabbed his backpack and entered the building. He walked past the wall of honor and was stopped by security at the small entrance to the building. The security guard did not recognize him, because he had grown a beard and it was seven months since he had visited HQ. Michael flashed his badge and the guy smiled and said sorry Mr. Vincent, Please proceed. He had arrived unannounced, so the receptionist had to call the director's office and tell him that Michael was in the house. The director told the receptionist to send him to his office immediately. Michael walked in and the director stood up and said" Glad to see you Michael, I was wondering if you would ever come back. Michael responded with a smile and said: "I was thinking seriously about it, but I know that there are always more things to be done., I think I am ready for another assignment." "Good Michael. We a very sensitive case." With that get picked up his phone and buzzed his secretary. "Susie please grab me the file C801 Make a copy and bring it to me."

Michael and the director chatted awhile, and he asked Michael how his sabbatical went. Fifteen minutes later while Michael was filling the director in on his past seven months, Susie came in and handed the director a folder. The director paced it a brown envelope and closed it, He then handed it to Michael and said." The reason this case is sensitive is because it is really the purview of the FBI and is a Stateside matter. However, you can do what they cannot. That is to eliminate an important threat to our country. Do you understand?" Michael understood he meant whack somebody and said yes Sir." All the information is in the folder, study it hard and then destroy its contents."

Michael put the folder in his laptop case, stood up shook   the director's hand and left his office. Michael left HQ and caught a taxi to Watermark hotel nearby. He had stayed there before and found it adequate. He checked into a patio room with a balcony and patio overlooking the city. It has a kitchenette, and the hotel has a full breakfast facility, bar, a pool, and a fitness center. It is all he needs for a short stay.

Michael settled in, and then went to the Bar to get himself a perfect Bourbon Manhattan on the rocks. He sat the bar and munched on some Trail mix while he enjoyed his drink. He then left the hotel and walked to a nearby restaurant called Amos Grill at 6271 Old Dominion DR.

He ordered Torshi for an appetizer (White wine & vinegar pickled carrots, cucumber, and cauliflower). For his main course he ordered Lamb chops with a wild berry sauce and Sour black cherries tossed with long grain basmati rice. He polished off a small carafe of red wine with dinner. He then returned to his hotel.

He changed into his T shirt and shorts and pulled out the envelope and sat down on his couch to read its contents.

The first page has a picture of a young Asian with the Name of Cheng Liu. His The following pages contain a Dossier that read as follows: "Born in Shanghai, entered the US five years ago and enrolled in the Illinois Institute of Technology in Chicago as an exchange student. He graduated with an electric engineering degree with a minor in Applied Mechanics and a second minor in Aerospace engineering. He then attended a masters accelerated program. After school he landed a job with Planet Labs in San Francisco, an Aerospace Company. He lives in China town.

He is identified as a Chinese spy that is suspected of stealing furnishing technology secrets from Planet Labs to another Chinese agent in China Town who travels back and forth to China as a businessman by the name of Zhen Feng importing Chinese food product." The last page was an explicit instruction to eliminate both. Michael thought (Wow, this one is going to be tough.) The following day he made a reservation on a business class flight from DC to Florida to visit his parents and pick up his clothes. After a two-day visit with his parents, he took a

United flight 1948 at 6:45PM from Florida to San Francisco.

CHAPTER 12   SAN FRANCISCO

When he arrived in San Francisco he took a taxi to the 845 California Apartments in China Town and rented a furnished apartment on the fourth floor. It was about 11:00 PM but he left the apartment and went to the 24-hour Cal-Mart store and bought some groceries. Butter Pecan rolls, cinnamon swirls. Bagels, butter, cold cuts and coffee. He also purchased a bottle of Bourbon, a bottle of sweet and dry vermouth. He then returned to his new apartment and retired for the night.

The following day he got up early in the morning and fixed himself a cup of coffee and ate some of the pastries he had purchased the night before. He then left the apartment, rented a car and took it to Plan-Labs for a streak out. He chose a spot to hang out in the park across the street from the entrance and exit doors of the building and parked his car there. It was about Eight thirty AM and Cheng Liu showed up for work.

Michael had packed himself a lunch of a cold cut sandwich on a bagel and a thermos of coffee. He sat in his car the entire afternoon, ate his lunch, and waited for his target to leave the building. At four thirty Cheng walked out of the building and got in a car. He backed out and drove away. Michael followed him to 680 Broadway to an apartment build and parked his car on the street outside. He got out and entered the apartment building. Michael knew now where Cheng lives. Michael waited about fifteen minutes and then he entered the building and checked the directory in the lobby. He saw the name of Chen Liu in apt 301. He made a mental note of that and left the building and returned to his apartment.

After he returned home, he made himself a perfect Bourbon Manhattan on the rocks, kicked off his shoes and sat down on the couch. He mentally planned his next day. He decided he would wait until Cheng left his apartment and then break into it to see what he could find. He then decided it was time to have dinner and he left the apartment and walked to a restaurant Mister Jiu's a Michelin star Chinese restaurant.

He sat down at a small table by the window and ordered Oysters on the half shell with apple, celery, and horseradish. For his main course he ordered Liberty farm Peking style Whole duck with house made pancakes, peanut butter hoisin, cucumbers, cilantro, and scallions. For dessert the Yogurt cream with ginger and puffed wild rice. With dinner he consumed a bottle of red wine.

After dinner he walked through China town and enjoyed the colorful lights, the hustle bustle of tourist and residents partaking in the evening bars, establishments, bars and food shops. He then returned to his apartment and went to bed.

The next day at Six AM he staked out Cheng's apartment and waited for him to leave. At seven thirty Cheng left his apartment. Michael waited until he was out of site and then he walked over to the apartment and entered the foyer. Instead of taking the elevator he walked up the back stairs to the third floor. He went straight to Apt 301 and picked the lock, and causally entered it. He made a quick survey and spotted a small desk with a computer in the living room. He opened the drawer of the desk and found a small address book. He took pictures of all the pages and returned them to the drawer. He then placed the sand disk in the computer and copied its contents. He then placed a bug in the telephone in the kitchen and left.

When Michael reached his apartment, he downloaded the sand disk to his computer. He found a recent message from Beijing to Cheng to destroy any evidence of his Military Research activities in China. It was in Chinese, but Michael was able to translate it with a translation program on site. Also told that whatever information he wanted to send to contact Zhen Feng.

Michael decided that he would stake out Cheng's apartment again the following day at four thirty PM. His hunch paid off and at five thirty PM Zhen showed up and entered Cheng's apartment. About a half hour later Zhen walked out of the building carrying a small package. Michael followed Zhen Feng to his direct tip to the Chinese Consulate. Zhen then left the Consulate twenty minutes later. Michael now had confirmation of their spy activity. Michael also had discovered an E-Mail from Cheng to Zhen to meet for dinner in three days at the Golden Dragon Restaurant for dinner.

Michael researched the Restaurant and found out it was owned by a member of the What Ching gang a rival of the Joe boys' gang. Michael thought this might be his opportunity. On the date of the dinner Michael stood across the street of the Golden Dragon and waited for Cheng and Zhen to emerge from the restaurant. It was about twelve midnight and Cheng and Zhen walked out, laughing and obviously somewhat plastered. Michael sprang into action dashed across the street and pumped two shots into each of them with his silencer. He then dropped a card he had made with the emblem of the Joe Boys and ran down the street away from the scene.

When he arrived home, he made himself a Perfect Manhattan on the rocks, sat down on his couch and turned on the TV. He tuned into the local Chinese channel and saw a report of police that were questioning people at the scene. The people were suspicious of the police and did not seem to cooperate. The next day the local newspaper had an article that had a headline" GANG SHOOTING

AGAIN AT GOLDEN DRAGON" The article went on to explain of then long-time rivalry of the two gangs and that one of the men was a merchant that may have been affiliated. Michael thought (Mission accomplished) The Police would be spending the next two weeks investigating a gang related crime.

Michael spent the next week just site seeing and enjoying the food of San Francisco. He took the cable car down to the turnaround at the wharf and walked to the Buena Vista and got himself their famous Irish coffee. The place was packed with friendly people and was amazed watching the bar tender Pouring 12 Irish coffees at the same time. He then walked to the wharf bought some sour dough bread and two large Dun genes crabs and had them shipped to his parents, because he knows how much they love it. He then took the cable car back up the hill to North beach and went to the North Beach Restaurant For dinner.

For his appetizer he ordered Scampi (three grilled baby Maine Lobster tails. For his next dish he got Gnocchi with Gorgonzola sauce. He then ordered Vitello Piccata (cooked in white wine, lemon, butter, and caper sauce. He ordered a bottle of 2011 Brunello di Montalcino. 0For dessert he got a Caffe di North Beach, Graffito coffee with the house five liquor blend topped with amaretto whipped cream. He was so filled he decide to walk back to China Town and his apartment.

 It was about eleven PM as he reached about two blocks from his apartment and three young Asian hoodlums on the prowl saw Michael, a white guy walking alone and thought he was an easy prey. They approached and circled him. Michael immediately took his karate stance and as they moved toward him, he hit one guy with a kick to the chest then swung around and hit the second guy with a kick to the head and then hit the third with a karate blow to the jaw. All three lay knocked out on the ground. Michael realized that his training had increased the effectiveness of his blows. He walked away slowly and left the three guys on the ground groaning and hurt badly but still alive.

Michael reached his apartment and packed up his things. He then called and made an airline reservation for the following day to fly back to DC. He notified the rental agent he was leaving and paid for the full month. The next morning, he drove his rental car to the airport and turned it in. He then caught a flight to the States.

CHAPTER 14   WASHINGTON DC

Michael arrived at Dulles International airport at 12:30 PM, at gate 63, terminal C. He was hungry and thirsty so when he walked off the plan, he stopped at the Vino Volo and sat down at the bar and got himself a Mediterranean Plate of olives, her bed goat cheese, roasted tomatoes, all drizzled with virgin olive oil and Crostini. He got a glass of French 2017 Gamay Noir, Henry Fesse. He then proceeded to the baggage area and collected his luggage.

He called CIA HQ and asked for the director of clandestine affairs office. He identified himself over the phone and was put through right away. The director picked up the phone and said "Welcome home Michael, please report in tomorrow at three PM for a debriefing. Come to the conference room on the top floor." "OK I will be there." Michael hung up and caught a taxi to take him back to the Watermark hotel. He checked into a small suite on the top floor. He unpacked and then went down to a bar for his afternoon perfect Bourbon Manhattan on the rocks.

The following morning, he got up at Seven AM, went to the fitness center for a one-hour workout followed by a twenty-minute swim in the pool. He then took a shower, dressed, and went to the buffet for breakfast. He relaxed in his room watching TV and reading the Newspaper o catch up on the events of the day. At 2:35 PM he took the elevator to the lobby and with his laptop case swung over his shoulder, he hailed a cab to take him to CIA HQ.

At 2:54 PM he walked out of the elevator on the top floor at HQ and walked briskly to the conference room. When he entered, he was met by the Director, Rossard, Joe Cicciano and an agent by the name of Marc who had recently returned from an assignment in Europe. They all stood up and greeted Michael with applause. He sat down and thanked them. He proceeded to give them a detailed account of his mission and turned over some of them additional information he had obtained from Cheng's apartment. He recommended that they check out all the people on the list for possible spy activity.

When Michael finished Rossard said "I know we have asked a lot of you, and you are thinking of retiring from field service. However, we have an important task that must be performed, and we cannot think of anyone better than you to carry it out." Joe chimed in and said, "We hope you would consider taking on another assignment." Michael hesitated and was silent for a couple of minutes then he said." What is it?"

The director said "The reason Marc has returned to the States is because he believes he was compromised and that his life is in danger. Eight US agents have been killed or are missing and we believe there is an unknown Russian Agent in Austria that is behind all the assassinations and disappearances." Marc said. "I had an informant that tipped me off that I was targeted". The Director chimed in again and said." This guy or woman who ever it is must be hunted down and eliminated. It seems anyone identified as part of the American Embassy as Marc was id targeted."

Joe said" It requires a lone wolf agent for this task, someone who could operate alone without back up. That's why we think you could be our best bet." "Michael responded "I Understand, OK I will take it on." With that answer, the director produced a brown envelope and placed it on the table in front of Michael. "Here Michael the envelope contains a first-class airline ticket to Vienna Austria, and 5,000 Euros for expense money We also have deposited $25,000 in an account in the Bank Austria, and a debit card that can be used at any of the many branches in Vienna. We also have made reservations for you at the Austria Trend hotel Savoyen Vienna." Rossard said "Your cover will be a Manufactures rep for an electronics firm by the name of US Electronics in St Louis. In the envelope are product brochures for the three main products. A ceramic Resonator, a Quartz Crystal Oscillator, and a quartz crystal. It also has information on the company's service and delivery policies. You can study them for a couple of days and take them with you to Vienna." "OK I got it gentlemen."

The meeting ended and Michael left the room with a new case of anxiety and went back to his hotel. He immediately went to the cocktail lounge and got himself a perfect Bourbon Manhattan on the rocks.

After an hour he decided to go to dinner, so he left the hotel and went a nearby local Italian Restaurant called Ristorante Buonarotti.

It is an upscale restaurant with white tablecloths, preset tables with silverware and glasses and an extensive wine menu. He ordered a cold appetizer of Prosciutto Parma Con Malone (Italian Prosciutto with melon). He ordered a small order of freshly made pasta with ground veal, cheese and bechamel, baked in a rich meat sauce. For his main course he ordered Agnolotti -Lamb, Lamb chop grilled and topped with a red Barolo wine sauce, served with Asparagus Bianchi Al Burro E Fromage (White asparagus with butter and Parmesan cheese sauce) and Patate con Erbe Jairo (Roasted potatoes with fresh herbs) With dinner he ordered a bottle of rare Italian red wine Allegrini Amarone. For dessert he drank a cup of Cappuccino "Bonaroti" (espresso, sambuca and whipped cream.) From the moment he entered Bonaroti he was treated like royalty and between the service and the excellent food it is one of the best Italian restaurants he ever ate at.

Full of a great meal, he decided to take a walk through the streets back to his hotel. It was a balmy evening, and the Moon was shining bright and bounced off the buildings of the city and over the landscape. As he walked along, he thought about the task ahead. His mind was already thinking of the things he might do in the future days. He reached his hotel and went straight to is room. He checked his envelope and saw that his flight was the following day at Six PM. This gave him time to prepare the next day, so he could get a good night s sleep and a workout in the morning, so he went to bed.

The following morning, he slept in until Nine O'clock, went to the fitness center, worked out for an hour, then took swim in the pool, had breakfast at the buffet. And returned to his room and took a shower. He then dressed, packed, and relaxed until lunch. He then had lunch sent to his room. At four PM he checked out and called a cab to take him to Dulles airport to catch his flight. He caught a quick sandwich and Beverage at the airport and then when it was time boarded the plane. He was able avoid security check in with his special pass and his diplomatic credentials. He took his seat in first class and he was immediately asked if he wanted something to drink. He responded with yes and asked for a perfect Bourbon Manhattan on the rocks and some peanuts. The Flight attendant was quick to honor his request and Michael settle in and relaxed for the flight.

During the 8 hour and 40 minutes flight Michael studied all the brochures on the products he is supposed to represent and memorized certain key facts. He managed to get some sleep and he was fed well and had all he wanted to drink. At seven thirty AM he was served breakfast and coffee. The flight was uneventful and landed in Vienna at Eight Forty AM.

CHAPTER 15   VIENNA AUSTRIA

There is a slight mist and light rain descending on the airport. He threw his laptop over his shoulder and departed the plane. When he picked up his bags, they were all wet.

Outside the terminal he went to a car rental agency desk and rented an Opel Corsa with a GPS. He put in the address of the hotel in the GPS and drove straight to it He checked in to Deluxe room that is laptop safe, has a min bar, desk and chair, couch, and a panoramic view of the city. He unpacked his clothes and placed them in the closet. It is about Ten thirty AM, and he went to the fitness center for his daily work out. He then showered and dressed. He decided to take a leisurely walk through the narrow cobblestone of Vienna. He passed numerous coffee shops and stopped to get a cup of coffee and a pastry. While he sat there drinking his coffee, he could see why an area like this a hot bed for foreign spies could be. He knows that based on Austrian BVT reports Austria and in particular Vienna is the house of hundreds of spies made up of many countries. Austria is one of the few friends in the EU of Russia and Putin even was a surprised guest at the Prime Minister's Daughter's wedding.

Michael finished his coffee and pastry and walked back to his hotel and went to his room. He took out his laptop and searched the internet for the address of the Russian Embassy. He found it at Reisner Strasse 45-7 1030 Wein. He also saw that there is an Embassy house, a four-story white building with a white metal fence around it with a large flagpole with the Russian flag. This building houses all the Russian diplomatic and agents. He decided that it would be a good place to stake out at. He also decided to place an AD in the local newspaper for his products, with a phone number to call.

Now was the time to sit and wait for response to his AD and for his surveillance attempts. Two days later he got a call from woman by the name of Anya Kolov. She said in English "interested in your product line can I meet you and talk about an arrangement.": Michael responded and said, "Yes meet me tomorrow evening at the Jazz club Zwe at 6:30 PM." "OK sir, I will be there. The Jazz club Zwe is one of the best clubs in Vienna and has a living room atmosphere, and top world-renowned Jazz Musicians.

At Three forty-five PM Michael strolled down to the Bar Soissen in the hotel and sat down at one of the12 Bar stools in the bar. He ordered his Perfect Bourbon Manhattan on the rocks and watched the bar change colors as the piano player played cool music in the corner of the room. He sat there until it was time to meet Anya at the Jazz club. He told her he would be wearing a white neckerchief, so she identified him. He arrived at Six twenty-five and took a seat at one of the plush couches in the room.

At Six thirty a glamorous red-haired women wearing a black leather pants suit and a red bandanna around her neck. Silver earrings hanging from her ears and carrying a leather brief case slung on her shoulder. She waked straight to Michael and said" Hi I am Anya, you must be Michael.": "Hello Anya, pleased to meet you, please sit down." She sat down on the couch opposite Michael, and he said." Can I order you a drink?" "Yes, that would be nice. I would like a Moscow mule." Michael motioned to the waiter and ordered her drink and a perfect Bourbon Manhattan on the rocks for himself. He also ordered a small plate of snacks to share.

While they were exchanging pleasantries and enjoying their drinks Anya opened the subject of the product line that Michael is supposed to represent. "I am very interested in purchasing your three main products for my company. Here is my card call me tomorrow and I will place the specific order and tell you where to ship it." 'OK, depending on the order, it will take about four weeks to ship" "OK that's fine" She then got up shook Michael's and left. As soon as she went through the door, Michael got up put fifty Euros on the table and hurried out the door to follow her.

She got in a Mercedes, and he jumped in his car and used his following skills to follow her a safe distance behind. As he thought she drove straight to the Russian Embassy house, passed through the gate, and disappeared. Michael no confirmed what he thought, she id a Russian agent and collecting information and product for Russia. The following day at Ten AM Michael called the number on the card and Anya answered in English. "Hello who is this?" "This is

Michael are you ready to place and order.?" "Yes, I would like to purchase fifty each of the three products. Ship them to The International electronics Corp Schikaneder Gasse 12, 1040 Wein Austria" "OK I will place your order right away."

Michael checked out the address and found it to be a warehouse for a company called International electronics Corp and a contact person by the name of Anya Sokolov. Since he had four weeks before he had to deliver a bogus order, he then decided to just provide surveillance on the Russian House. For the next three days he hung out across for the Russian Embassy house. On the third day he saw Anya leave the Embassy and go to the park where there is a memorial statue of a Russian Hero. As she waited at the site, an unknown individual showed up and met her in the park. Michael took pictures of them both as she passed on to him a package with documents.

Michael decided to follow the unknown individual and he led him to a Villa in Vienna. The following day he staked out the villa and at about ten PM the individual left the villa and went to a location across from the American Embassy. The Russian was waiting for an

American agent to leave the Embassy. Michael instinctively knew this guy must the Russian assassin, waiting to make a kill. At about eleven PM an American Diplomat left the embassy on his way home. Michael saw the Russian drew a silencer and took aim on the American. Before the guy could get off a shot, Michael reached down and pulled out his boot knife and threw it and hit the guy in the chest. He then pulled out his silencer and pumped two shots in the fallen Body. Michael retrieved his knife and then made a b-line for his hotel.

When he reached the hotel, he went straight for the Bar and cocktail lounge. He got himself a perfect Bourbon Manhattan on the rock, to calm himself down. He thought this was a close call. He now had a couple of weeks before he had to deliver the bogus order. He also decided that Anya is also a threat, and he should eliminate her.

The following day he called her and told her that there is some complication her order, that he is sure he could work thing out. Can she meet him at Six PM at the Bar Saissons for drink to discuss things. She agreed and at six she walked in the door and over to

Bar where Michael was sitting. He had ordered her a Moscow Mule which is sitting there waiting for her. When no one was looking he managed to place a slow-effective poison pill in her drink. Unaware She thanked him for the drink and Michael proceed to tell her that there would be a delay on the shipment, but he is going to tell his company to set a priority on the order.

She thanked him, finished her drink, and left the Bar. She got in her Mercedes and drove off. Ten Minutes later she passed out drove car into a lamp pole. When the police arrived at the scene, she not only was passed out, but she was dead from the undetectable poison. Michael went to his room and packed up his things and checked out of the hotel. He drove his car to the airport and caught a flight to Paris.

CHAPTER 16   PARIS FRANCE

The flight arrived at Charles De Gaulle airport at 6:15
PM and he caught a taxi to take him to his favorite
hotel, the hotel Loti at 7 Rue de Castiglione. He tipped
the taxi driver, and a bellhop met him at the door and
carried his bags to the reception desk. The pretty
brunette receptionist recognized Michael and said"
Welcome back Mr. Vincent, it's good to see you
again" "Thank you Ms. Do you have a room with a
balcony?" "Yes sir" She handed him the keys to a mini
suite on the top floor. The bell hop helped him with
his luggage to the room and asked him if there is
anything he could do for him. He Said No Thank you
and he tipped the Bellhop.

Michael unpacked and then made a phone call To
Cynthia. She answered the phone and said" Hello
Who's this?" "It's Michael Cyn, I am in Paris. I just
arrived at my hotel and would like to see you." "You
Bastard, I thought you were dead, or forgot me." "No
Cyn, I just have been on a number of assignments and
could not contact you." "When can I see you,

Michael?" "I made a reservation for the two of us for a Maxim's dinner cruise on the Seine for tomorrow night. Can you make it?" "Yes, what time?" Pick me up at the Lotti hotel art 6:45 PM. WER must board the boat at 7:30 PM." "OK Michael, see tomorrow night." Michael hung up the phone and took the elevator down to his favorite Bar and cocktail lounge. He walked in and for the first time was aware of the beautiful Baroque Decor with masterpiece paintings on the walls, a bar and bar stools like they were from the 1930's. The room was dimly lit and comforting atmosphere. He sat down on one of the plush bar stools and ordered his Perfect Bourbon Manhattan on the rock. He was totally relaxed and anxious to see Cynthia the following day.

As he sipped his drink, he thought maybe it's time to give up the clandestine life and settle down. He Thought that the last mission was a close call, and his luck may run out. He might become a star on the wall of honor. He was thankful that he had managed to accumulate a sizable amount of funds which he had tucked away in the bank in Monte Carlo. He was so content now he ordered a second drink and sat there enjoying the surroundings. At about Eleven PM he retired to his room and got some sleep.

The next morning, he got up at Seven AM, put on his sweats and went for a run through the streets of Paris. There was a morning mist that started to lift off the city and the sun started to take hold. By the time he had been running for an hour he had worked up a good sweat. He returned to his room, took a shower, dressed, and then went down for the breakfast buffet. He then left the hotel and took a cab to the Louvre Museum, spent three hours viewing the many paintings and sculptures. He was surprised to see how small the Mona Lisa painting is. When he left the Museum, he stopped at a small sidewalk cafe and got himself a glass of wine and a Ham sandwich. He sat there and people watched while he ate his lunch. On the way back to his hotel he stopped and bought a bottle of Cynthia's favorite perfume and had it gift wrapped.

Michael spent the rest of the day relaxing and watching TV, Then at Five PM He took another shower, dressed in a pair of designer jeans, black turtleneck shirt and his grey swede jacket. He slipped on his black boots and went down to the lobby waiting for Cynthia to pick him up. Her black Limo pulled up and the driver got out and opened the door to the back seat. Michael got in and gave her a hug. She was kind of aloof, which surprised Michael. She said glad to see you Michael and you are in good shape as usual." "You look great" She was dressed in a black V neck velvet cocktail dress with black pumps, a diamond necklace around her neck and earrings to match. They glistened in the twilight of the evening.

They arrived at the barge boat at just the right time of Seven twenty-eight PM. Michael helped her on to the boat and they were escorted to table on a window with a paramedic view. The boat was dimly lit, and a Jazz Piano is playing jazz classics. As they sat down the were greeted with a waiter that served them glasses of French Champaign and Appetizers.

As the boat cruised down the river, it passed the Eiffel tower lit up in all its splendor, the Arc de Triumph, and all the glistering buildings reflecting on the water. Cynthia asked Michael many questions about his past experiences, and He was careful to tell her only select information. They dined on Foie Gras from the harvest, with apple chutney and spices, then Grenadine of Veal Morels, and sweat potato Mousseline, and the Champaign was served constantly. During dinner Michael gave her the perfume. She thanked him and said, "You should not have done that." The dinner cruise ended at 10:15 PM and the boat docked. Waiting for them was Cynthia's Limo, they got in and the driver took them back to Michael's hotel. When they arrived, Michael was about to invite her up to his room, but before he could do it, she said "Michael I have something to tell you. First thank you for dinner and all the good times we had together, but this is the last time we will ever see each other again. I could not wait for you to be a permanent part of my life and in your absence. I met somebody, and I am engaged to be married." Michael slumped down in the seat and the final rejection hit him hard. She wished him luck and a good life. The driver opened the door, and he got out and walked slowly into the lobby. Instead of going to his room he went to the Bar and got himself a double perfect Manhattan on the rocks and tears rolled down his cheeks.

He was sad, regretful, mad at himself, as well as many other feelings. He reflected on how she had been such an important part of his life. The next morning, he woke up at 9:00A, rubbed his eyes and realized that he had slept all night on the couch. He for minute he did not realize what had transpired the night before and then it him again.

As he drank a cup of coffee on the balcony, he started to think what he would do next. As he sipped his coffee the clouds moved in, and it started to rain. It was as so the heavens were crying over his situation. Michael clears his head with a walk. He put on his raincoat, and fisherman's hat and left the hotel and left the hotel. He walked down to the river and walked along the pouring rain. His mood matched the day and the water hit his face as he walked. Since the weather is so dismal, Michael is the only person out at about on his sweats. He then returned drenched, tired, and rejected he returned to the hotel. He took a warm shower and called the airlines and booked a flight back to the states for the following day. He sent a coded message to CIA HQ that read "Red wave is stopped, and White Rose is off the vine." (Translated meant

Russians assassinated and he is now coming in from the cold for good.") When the section chief got the message, he had mixed emotions. Elated that the mission was accomplished but not happy that Michael is throwing in the towel. He shot back a message to Michael come and visit me again before you pack it in." Michael responded "OK."

CHAPTER 17   BACK IN THE USA

The Air France plane descended through the thick white clouds and reveled the land on the seat belt sign and below. The pilot turned and announced their final descent. Fifteen minutes later the plane landed at Dulles airport in DC. Michael collected his luggage and caught a taxi to take him to Langley. When he arrived, he carried a laptop over one shoulder and his garment bag over the other. He had shipped one bag to his Parents in Florida with a note that he would soon see them.

Michael announced his arrival and was told to go to seventh floor conference room. He took the elevator and walked down the long corridor to the conference room. He was met by a secretary and told to wait in the room. He waited about fifteen minutes and suddenly the two oak great doors to the room opened and in walked about two dozen people including the director Of the CIA. He was carrying a red velvet box. They filled the seats in the room, and some stood along the perimeter of the room.

The director stood at the head of the table and made a small speech welcoming Michael and asked him to join him at the end of the room. With that he reads a document of praise and accomplishment. With that he opened the box and took out a The National Intelligence Exceptional Achievement Medal and hung it around Michael's neck. Michael was flabbergasted, it is an award only bestowed by the director of the CIA and is rarely given. He then pinned the ribbon on Michael's jacket. With that as if on Que the door opened again, and they reeled in a cart with a big cake and bottles of Champaign with glasses. The room exploded with applause and each on congratulated Michael as they toasted his success.

When the meeting was over the director thanked him for his service and told him to stay in touch. Michael left the room with his Medal in the red velvet box which he had tucked away in his laptop case. He then felt that a burden had been lifted off his shoulders and was now free to go about his business as he wished. He decided to take the train to Florida to visit his aging parents.

While on the train, he took out the medal to take a close look at it. It is silver colored oval. On the obverse of the medal, at the top is a scalloped design with seven raised sections, from top to down to the sides. In the center is a gold heraldic rose with a gold disc superimposed over it bearing a compass rose. At the base of the medal is a gold olive wreath. The reverse bears the words NATIONAL INTELLIGENCE EXCEPTIONAL ACHIEVEMENT in four lines. This is above where Michael's name is engraved. He thought (Wow, this something.) He put it away and decided to go to the cocktail bar and once again reminisced about Cynthia. He drank his afternoon Perfect Bourbon Manhattan on the rocks while clicking of the train tracks seem to put out a memorizing spell. He was looking forward to seeing his parents and having a home cooked meal.

When the train arrived in Orlando, he rented a car and drove to his parents' home. He pulled into their driveway and rang the bell. His mother came to the door and was shocked to see her son standing there. She dropped her apron and gave him a big hug. She yelled for his father who walked slowly to front door.

He too gave Michael a big hug and was pleasantly surprised to see him Michael's mother said "You are\ just in time for dinner" she told Michael to put his bags in his room. He then returned to the kitchen where his father was about to open a bottle of Barolo for dinner.

Michael said What's for dinner mom?" Veal cutlet, stuffed eggplant, and a salad. Michael's dad poured a glass of wine for himself, and Michael poured a glass of chardonnay for Michael's Mother. mother continued to While he prepares dinner Michael, and his father had an update kind of conversation. He Asked Michael about where he had been. Michael told him about the places but not what did there.

During dinner his mother wanted to know if he had met woman, he is interested in. He said, "Not any one special yet Mom." Michael enjoyed the warmth of his family and his mom's cooking. For dessert she had Italian cookies and black coffee. During dessert Michael said I have some to show you. He got up and went to the bedroom and fetched his medal. He put the red velvet box on the table and his father opened it. He said "Holy cow Michael This is wonderful I am impressed. I know how important and rare award this is, we are proud of you" Michael returned it to box and spoke. "Mom and this to add to my collection.

Michael spent the next week with his parents enjoying the chats, food, and bottles of wine. He knew that the time would come for him to leave, and it would be hard on his parents as well as for him. That day came and he gave them both a big hug and said his goodbye. They stood in the driveway waving to him with tears in their eyes as he drove away. Michael drove to the Orlando airport and caught a flight to San Francisco.

CHAPTER 24   THE PRESIDIO

At his request he got the CIA to approve his attendance at the Military Defense Language school at the Presidio. He rented a car and drove 120 miles south of San Francisco to the Monterey Peninsula and entered the gates of the Presidio. He checked in at the registration building and is signed up for the combination Chinese Mandarin and Russian language program. The Chinese Mandarin program is a 64-week course, and the Russian program is a 45-week course. Both courses teach students to a high level of proficiency and instructional methods are focused on a mixed method approach, utilizing interactive teaching activities. Topics go far beyond conventional foreign language courses, treating the in-depth exploration of issues related to history, geography, politics, economy, society, and culture.

Michael went to class five days a week for seven hours a day and had to do two to three hours of homework each night. It was the most intense academic training he ever encountered. His classes were small with only 4 to 5 people and an instructor. He is housed in a bachelor's Quarter at the Navy lodge in La Mesa Villa. It has a fully equipped kitchenette, TV, free newspaper each day, free in-room coffee, and access to a complimentary breakfast.

Michael is impressed with the Presidio. It contains over 1000 classrooms and faculty facilities, 50 computer labs, 8 advanced computer language labs, a library of films, periodicals, and material. Michel his studies settled in and went at with a vengeance. Since most of the students were in one of the military branches and had to do physical training along with their studies, Michael did not have to but decided to join the Army unit to train with them. All students wore a uniform without rank insignia, so no one knew the rank or position of the classmate.

On the weekends, for a little bit of relaxation Michael would travel across the Golden Gate Bridge to Sausalito. Once a month he would treat himself to a meal at one the famous fish restaurants in Sausalito. His first place was called The Franciscan. He started off with a Dungeness crab Caesar salad, He then ordered a dish of Crab Fettuccine Alfredo. and a half bottle of Antinori Christina Pinot Grigio. from Sicily. He enjoyed the restaurant so much sitting outside and overlooking the bay, he returned the next month and got himself Their world-famous Whole Killer Crab. (A hot Dungeness Crab, in their secret Garlic sauce.)

Throughout his time at the Presidio, he would go to Sausalito often for a Gelato, lunch, dinner, or shopping in the many shops. When he was studying Chinese, he would go to San Francisco China town listen to the people speak in Chinese and Mandarin dialect. For more than a year and a half it was a combination of hard study, pleasant outings and engaging with other students.

It finally came to an end and he left then Presidio with two more languages under his belt. He decided that he would no longer get instructions from HQ, but he would travel the world and seek his own opportunities to fight against enemies of the USA at the same time live as luxuriously as possible. He wanted to put his newly learned Chinese language to use so he booked a flight to Taiwan because he knew from Intel reports that there are about 5K Chinese spies in the country infiltrating the Government and recruiting civilians.

CHAPTER 19   TAIPEI TAIWAN

The untied Airline flight 871 landed at 6:45 PM from San Francisco at the Zhongshan Airport in Taipei. Michael exited the plane after the long flight. He had to go through customs but did not declare anything and showed is US passport. He was asked the purpose of his trip and Business and holiday. He responded part business and part holiday. They let him enter and he entered the baggage area and collected his bags. He took a taxi to the Mandarin Oriental Taipei hotel. It is one of the best hotels in Taiwan. It has a full-service spa, outdoor and indoor pool, massage treatment rooms, fitness center, three restaurants, one French, one Italian and one Asian. It also has a cocktail lounge and bar.

Michael signed into a small Bedroom suite with a balcony and a view of the city. Since it was about Seven thirty PM and he decided to go to the bar and get his evening Cocktail, so he went to the BO bar. It was most elegant lounge and bar he had.

encountered so far. There was a very attractive female bar tender as well as with a young Asian man. She took his order with a big smile and made him his perfect Bourbon Manhattan on the rocks.

As he sat and enjoyed the atmosphere and his drink at the beautiful bar, he realized that all the people obviously very affluent Asians as well as international guest. After his drink, Michael decided to go to dinner at Ya Ge Asian restaurant in the hotel. When the waiter came to take his order, he spoke to him in Mandarin. He ordered Plum wine meat aspic for an appetizer, He then ordered Cherry Duck. Peking style, slow roasted, he then ordered braised Abalone with Oyster sauce. For dessert he got Mango, Pomelo, with Sago cream. He drank a half bottle of dry white Changyu wine. The meal was a five-star Asian meal and he decided he would frequent the restaurant during his stay.

After dinner he retired to his room for a good night's sleep. In the morning at seven AM Michael went to the fitness center and worked out for about an hour. He then went to the indoor pool and took a swim. He then got himself pampered at one of the 12 private treatment rooms for a hot stone massage and body rub. He then returned to his room, took a shower, and dressed.

He then took a tax to the American Embassy to pick his small metal clandestine case which he had shipped via diplomatic courier. When he arrived at the Embassy, he showed his special credentials from the CIA, and he was escorted to the Station chief office. They chatted for a while, and he notified him that he was on a private mission and did not need back up. He also told them that he is traveling throughout Asia and is aware that there are 5000 Chinese spies in Taiwan. He left the embassy and returned to his hotel with his case. He then opened it up and took out his boot knife and camera glasses. He relaxed until early evening, and he then hit the streets and took the green line 3 to Zhongshan station, took exit 3 to the street and the Nao hoe night market. Michael strolled through the market and tasted the mouthwatering local delicacies such as an oyster omelet, barbecued sausage, braised duck tongue walking the streets with picture of the former student in his mind.

One night he was sitting at a jazz bar in the night market and in came two Chinese guys and they were laughing and kibitzing and tipsy. Michael recognized one of them as the missing former student. As they passed Michael's small table one of them bumped into Michael and said in Mandarin. "You're in my way white guy" Much to their surprise Michael responded in Chinese Mandarin ": Watch where you are going you Idiot." He purposely tried to be provocative. He sat finished his drink and then got up and walked out.

As he predicted the two guys followed him outdoors. The night was late, and the narrow street was quiet. Michael was aware that they had come out and was following him.

When they reached a dark part of the cobblestone street, Michael turned around and the two guys were within six feet, and they charged him shouting "We will teach you a lessen you American Pig. Michael intermediately took a Karate stance. As they both approached, he hit one with a blow in the bridge of his nose and whirled around and kicked the side of the head of the other. Both lay moaning on the ground. He then took out his boot knife and slit the throats of both. He took pictures of them lying dead and then he returned to his hotel.

The next morning, he went to breakfast and then then went to the outdoor pool to relax. He took a short swim to cool off and then laid down in of the Lounge chairs. While he was lounging on one of the chairs, a good-looking Chinese waiter came up him and said, "Can I get you anything sir?" "Yes, Miss you can. I want something refreshing. Please bring me a Green Goddess cocktail and a snack. "Ten minutes later she returned with his drink and a small platter with an assortment 2 each of a fried crab spring roll, pickled in brine pot stewed Duck neck, and Sashimi an ancient, traditional pastry of Beijing (Egg and flour, fried in hot honey.

Michael said "Thank you Miss" in Mandarin and she smiled and walked away. Michael enjoyed the cool drink and the great snacks. Periodically he would jump in the pool and take a swim. He observed that there few very attractive young Asian women also lounging around the pool. He was tempted to try and engage with one of them but thought twice of it. He thought to himself, they must have rounded up all the beautiful

Chinese women and brought them to this hotel. They were everywhere, the staff, and the guests, wherever he went.

After he had enough of the poolside, Michael returned to his room and dressed to go out. He caught a taxi and asked the driver to take him to the Forge of Ron Chen the sword maker. It took about twenty-five minutes to get there, and Michael asked the driver to wait. Michael walked int the foundry and Ron Chen was busy at working on his next masterpiece., Las luck would have it the sword maker was at a point where he could stop in the process. He greeted Michael with "Can I help you? "Michael said "Yes sir, I saw your Shi Tanto was available for purchase and I would like to buy it." "OK, I will get it" He went over to a cabinet at the end of the room and pulled out a twenty-inch Brown velvet box and opened it. It was just as Michael expected.

It was of high quality and made in the same tradition of the companion Katana. The Hamon (temper line) on the forged steel blade is prominent in the polish. There are two narrow groves carved in the back of the blade. A matching Kozuka (knife) is also featured as part of the Tanto. A rain Motif is etched in the Habaki. Michael took out his credit card and paid $1100 for the Tanto. He also ordered a companion Shi Shi Katana companion piece to be made and shipped to his parents' home. This would take three months and cost him another three thousand dollars, which he also paid for in advance with the credit card. He then thanked Ron and left the forge, got in the cab and had the driver take him back to the hotel.

It was late afternoon when he got into his hotel so after he dropped off his purchase in his room, he went to the bar to get his afternoon Perfect Bourbon Manhattan on the rocks. He sat at the bar and people watched while he sipped his drink. After a while he decided to go to dinner the Italian restaurant Bencotto in the hotel'

Here he ordered Polpo Alla Griglia (grilled octopus with potato gnocchi), for his pasta he ordered Tagliatelle All'Astice (Tagliatelle with butter poached lobster and coral sauce), and for his next dish he got roasted Yilan duck breast, turnip, pickled cherries, Polenta, duck jus. For his dessert he eats Tiramisu Affogato (Tiramisu sphere, grappa gelato, espresso.)

He topped his meal with a half-bottle of vintage Tignanello

Michael spent the next few days enjoying Taipei and decided it was time to move on. He found out that the city of Macau China was the gambling capital off the Southern coast China.

CHAPTER 20   MACAU CHINA

At Seven AM Michael got up, packed his things, checked about, and caught a taxi outside the hotel to take him to the airport. He bought passage on a Mandarin flight to Macau at 10:35 AM. He checked his bags and boarded his first-class seat. As soon as he was seated a good-looking flight attendant asked him if she could get him something. He asked her for a cup of coffee and a pastry. She promptly accommodated him. Since there are no nonstop flights, he had to land in Faohing island with a two hour and forty-five minutes stay over until is next flight to Macau. His flight to Macau arrived at six thirty PM.

At Macau International they caught an airport Limo to take him to the "City of Dreams Macau hotel. As the Limo dove to the hotel, Michael was amazed at the many hotels and casinos, and he thought it rivaled Las Vegas. He was in awe as the limo pulled up to his hotel. Although the Venetian hotel and casino is the largest in the world and a copy of the Venetian in Las

Vegas, the City of Dreams is smarter, younger and hipper.

The resort is a beautiful combination of sweeping artistic interiors, bold lighting, and contemporary furnishing while accommodation and dining are in abundance. It is a place where one can relax and become comfortable as well as empty your wallet. He registered and got the keys to Rom with a king size bed and a balcony. The room is fitted with an Ottoman and marble bathroom with a walk-in shower, mini bar and a safe. It is Seven PM by the time he was settled in, dressed in a clean pair of jeans, a red turtleneck shirt, his leather jacket and he went down to the cocktail lounge and bar. He walked into the bar with high ceilings, a big glass lit arch behind the bar and an arch within the big arch with lighted shelves holding all the bottles of liquor. He sat down at one of the five stools at the bar and ordered his Perfect Bourbon Manhattan on the rocks.

After finishing is drink, he went to the Jade Dragon three-star Michelin Chinese restaurant for dinner. He was met by statuesque tall, beautiful woman dressed in a silk patterned long dress with a split up the side that exposed her long legs when she walked. She smiled and said follow me sir. He said thank you in Mandarin, and she handed him a menu and he sat down at a table that was preset and at a window.

For an appetizer he ordered Wok fried crispy soft-shell crab with spices and pepper. He then got an order of whole supreme Yachihama Abalone, an order of Australian Lobster (cooked, raised with yellow pepper sauce, baked in supreme sauce steamed with garlic and baked with ginger and spring onion. Stir fried with truffle an in white Mirin sauce then backed with chestnut butter, served with rice. After dinner he returned to his hotel room, changed into his PJ's, and watched a little TV, and went to bed.

The next morning Michael put on pair of shorts, a T shirt and sneakers and went for a run on the Coati strip with seeing all the casinos along the way. He thought it is like being in Las Vegas. His run lasted about a half hour and a half hour back to his hotel. He then went to his room, put on his swim trunks and the bath robe and went for a swim in the hotel pool.

After his swim, he dressed and went to Breakfast and then decided to go see the action packed and unique water-based show in the casino. It was part synchronized swimming, and a part Evil Knievel type breathtaking spectacle. After the show he proceeded to floor of the casino to do some gambling. He walked over to a crap table and There is a full table of people. One guy left the table and Michael slipped in his spot. An elderly Chinese guy has the dice, and he rolls a five. He then rolls a snake eye and loses. He passed the dice to a good-looking Asian woman Michael bet one hundred dollars on her winning and she roils a seven and they both win. He then took the dice and bet another hundred and rolled an eleven and won then he doubled up and rolled again. This time it was eight. He rolled again and hit his number and won again. He noticed that the Good-looking Asian woman left the table, so he gave up his dice and followed her. She went straight to the roulette table. Michael purchased a thousand dollars of chips and waited to see to place a bet. He had a feeling that she was lucky so he would ride her bet. She put five $100 chips on odd red, and Michael did the same. The wheel turned and landed on 3 red. The next bet She placed another $500 Even black. Michael put $1000 worth of chips on even black. The wheel turned and landed on 4 black. Michael thought I better quit while I'm ahead, so he cashed in his chips and walked away with $25,000. He then left the casino and went to dinner at the Yi Restaurant.

He took the elevator to the 21st floor sky bridge and entered the golden metal walled entrance way and was seated at one of white clothed covered tables near the large window. Ne room was ultra-modern design with sweeping curved white and golden metal motif that swept all the way to the ceiling. The waiter came to his table to take his order and made a recommendation, which he accepted.

He ordered the Trio of Cantonese, Yellow croaker, Iberico, and chicken roll. Then he ordered Abalone with blue shrimp, clams, and rice in a lobster sauce. He also ordered roasted pigeon with lemon grass and a Carafe of Meursault Pierre-Boisson. He topped the meal off with a glass of Cognac. He then left the restaurant and took the elevator down to his floor and entered his room. He spent the rest of the week pampering himself in the great lifestyle and then decided he should move on.

He was very lucky at the casino and wired about $100,000 to his bank account. He returned to s room to relax. He took out is laptop and searched the news. He saw a news article about Russian spies performing espionage on a Norwegian armor depot by blowing it up. The article went on to say the authorities have been hunting for the ringleader of a spy's cell living in Helsinki. Michael thought about it and decided that he would get back in the game and would go to Norway to hunt down the Russian Spy.

The next morning, he packed up, checked out and caught a taxi to the airport. He booked a flight at 7:45PM on Juneyao airline to Shanghai Pudong International airport and arrived at 8:55 AM. He had to stay over and then changed planes to a Finn air flight to Helsinki, which arrived at 4:05 PM.

CHAPTER 21 HELSINKI FINLAND

When he arrived in Helsinki, he rented a Volvo with a GPS system. To pick up the car he had to go to the garage at the airport to space 38. As he walked through the garage to find his car, he notices About ten percent of the cars parked were up scale luxury and sport cars with Russian license plates. He found out later wealthy Russians it and its license plate. He then found his rental, set the GPS for the address of his hotel, threw his bags in it and drove it out of the garage.

Michael arrived at the Lapland Hotel Bulevardi and found it to be in an excellent location. It's near several attractions and a short walk to the Kamppi shopping center and near the bus terminal. Michael was met by a valet attendant who took his car and a doorman who took his luggage into the lobby and to the registration desk Michael booked a Mystique Deluxe room with French balcony. His room was on the top floor and a bellboy helped him to his room.

The room included a desk, safe, flat screen TV, and a sauna. The bathroom contained a design bath and shower, bathrobe, and terry cloth slippers. Michael unpacked and went down Bar in the hotel for his afternoon perfect bourbon Manhattan on the rocks. After he finished his drink, he moved to a table in the Kulta restaurant where he was presented with a menu by a waiter. He selected Lapland delicacies (consisting of northern fish, reindeer, forest mushrooms, farm cheese Lappish berries), for his appetizer. He then ordered sauteed Reindeer with mashed Lappish potatoes, pickled cucumber, and berries. He selected a half bottle of Sanhsaa Piemontre Barbera Appassimento. (Marchesi Di Barolo) He then ordered a cheese selection with cloud berry jam and a cup of coffee. It was now about Eight thirty, so he went to his room for the evening. The following morning, he went down to the fitness center and worked out for an hour and a half and worked a good sweat. He then returned to his room stripped down and took hot sauna, a cold showered, dressed and returned to the restaurant for a Nordic Breakfast of hot Bilberry Oat porridge, Scrambled eggs with smoked salmon and fruit, Brown cheese, Norwegian bread, and coffee.

After breakfast Michael went to the lobby and asked the attendant to fetch his car. When his car arrived, he tipped the Attendant and drove away. He headed for the airport and drove into the garage. He drove around until he found the Bentley with the Russian plate and medallion. He found it in a different place, and he parked his car close by where he could observe anyone getting in the Russian car. His stake out lasted about three hours when a Middle-aged gray hair man walked over to the car opened the trunk and threw his bag and what looked like an attaché case into the trunk and closed it.

The Russian got in the car and drove out of the garage, with Michael in close pursuit. Michael expected the Russian to drive to the Russian Embassy but his was surprised that the guy drove to a park where there is a statue of a Russian war hero. There he parked his car and waited. Suddenly a young woman walked up to the Russian's car, and he opened his window. She Took out a large envelope from her brief case and handed it to the guy in the car. Michael took pictures of the transaction and special pictures of the woman.

Michael was faced with a dilemma on whether to follow the guy in the car or the woman. He knew that the Russian car would go to the embassy, so he decided to follow the woman. She walked across the street and got in a car. Michael hen followed that car and took a picture of the license plate which is a Finland license plate. Michael concluded that she is a resident spy. He followed her to the neighborhood of Kallio, the hipster and student district village of Helsinki. It's only a short tram ride to town center and is a much relaxed and has a cool hip atmosphere. The hipster atmosphere gives Kallioa a somewhat a bad reputation in the rest of the city, but young people flock to the area to make it their home. It is also the perfect place where a young Russian spy could become part of a diverse culture scene.

She parked her car and walked into a burnt red color three story apartment house with two big windows on the ground floor and a bicycle leaning against the building. Michael made note of the address and took multiple pictures of it. He waited until it was about twelve thirty in the afternoon and she emerged dressed in jeans, a sweatshirt and a red bandanna around her head. She started walking so Michael got out of his car and followed her.

She stopped at the Savel Bar and Bistro and met two young men outside. They exchanged greetings and entered the Bistro. Since the scene was filled with people, Michael was able to follow them into the Bar and Bistro without much suspicion. They sat down at a table and ordered a round of Beer. They also apparently ordered something to eat. Michael sat down at a table facing them and very nearby. Then he took pictures of the group with his eyeglass camera. The waiter approached Michael and asked him if he could get him something. He said, "Yes sir please bring me a glass of Helsinki Bryggeri IPA Beer, and an order of fried liver with lingonberry sauce."

The waiter left the table and Michael took out his directional pen recorder and turned it on and placed it in his shirt pocket. Michael ate his lunch, drank his beer, and then followed the three targets out of the Savel bar and Bistro. They walked to the University and walked into the building that housed the classrooms. Michael now knows that they are all students. Michael returned to his car and drove back to his hotel. When he arrived at the hotel he went to his room and loaded the pictures on his laptop and played the recorder and listened attentively. They were speaking in Russian and Michael's Russian training came in handy. He heard them talking about a plan to blow up a Finish Naval facility and that they would pattern it after the Armor dept they were successful in accomplishing.

Michael now realized that he had to take out all three of them. The woman leader told them to meet her at the park with the Russian Hero statue the following night at Eleven PM and they would drive together to the Naval facility. Michael then droves to her apartment and arrived at Ten PM. He then walked to her car and paused. He looked around and there was none around. He placed an explosive device under the car and then drove to the park and waited.

At Eleven sharp the three arrived at the park and after talking a few minutes they all got in the Woman's car. As they drove slowly away from the park, Michael pressed the button of the detonator, and the car blew the car to smithereens and burst into flame. The explosive was intensified by the explosive in the car that was planned to be used in their Naval base blow up. He the sped away and drove straight to his hotel and to his room. He opened his mini bar a took out a mini bottle of bourbon, poured it into a glass with some ice and sat down on his couch and sighed. He was sweating with nerves and although he was positive that he did Finland a favor, he would not be able to let them know what he did. After he finished his drink, he went to bed and watched some TV. He saw a news broadcast and there are fire trucks on the sight of the Michael fell asleep and the TV was still going.

The next morning Michael got up went to the fitness center and worked out for an hour. He then returned to his room, took a shower and dressed to go to breakfast. He ate a typical Finnish breakfast. He decided that he needed take a break from his crusade against terrorist and spend some time in a cultural experience related to his Sicilian heritage. He checked out of the hotel and drove his rental car to the airport and turned it in. He then booked his flight to Palermo. It is a multi-city stop flight From Helsinki to Amsterdam to Milan to Punta Raisi airport in Palermo Sicily.

CHAPTER 22   PALERMO SICILY

Michael collected his bags and went straight to the car rental counter in the terminal. He rented a Fiat 500 compact SUV with a GPS. When he picked up his car, he set the GPS for the Grand Hotel Et Des Palmas at Via Roma 398 90139. When he arrived, he drove up to the Baroque building with an elegant entrance way he was met by a doorman in a red suit with gold buttons and a red bellboy cap. He opened the door for Michael and helped him unload his luggage onto a luggage cart. He then took Michael's keys and gave him a ticket for valet service. He then led Michael to the registration desk. Michael tipped the Doorman and said "Grazia" The doorman said "Prego."

Michael booked a special room with a balcony and a view of Palermo Harbor in the distance. The hotel and its rooms are decorated in elaborate Baroque Style. Since it was late afternoon, he had settled into his room he went down to the elegant cocktail lounge and bar. He sat down at one of the plush bar stools and ordered his Perfect Bourbon Manhattan on the rocks.

The bar tender is one of the worlds expert mixologists, so Michael did not have to explain on how to make his drink. Bar tender said "Si Signore" The bartender proceeded to take a metal cocktail mixer, pour two jiggers of Bourbon, a half jigger of sweet vermouth, a half jigger of dry vermouth. And some ice. He shook it vigorously and poured it to a tumbler glass over ice and then added Biters to the drink and handed it to Michael. The drink was made with high quality Italian vermouth and a very expensive Bourbon. It was the best Perfect Bourbon Manhattan that Michael ever had. He then moved on to the restaurant in the hotel for dinner. He ordered Scallops coked in almond milk with chi orzo for his appetizer and then Raviolo with Mussels in olive oil and sesame purple shrimp for his second course and then Beef of Veal with a special black truffle and chocolate meat sauce.

The following morning Michael Went down to the Grand Ballroom where the hotel served breakfast every day. He ate a typical Sicilian breakfast of almond pastries, Granita crushed ice, and coffee. After breakfast he set out to do some site sightseeing in

Palermo. His first stop is the Palace of Normans sometime called the Royal Palace, in the Piazza Independenza. The Palace is a mix of the various cultures that built it.

His next stop is the Palermo Cathedral down the street. He walked down to the first row opposite the altar and sat down. His eyes took in its unique architecture and how it is a true melting pot of styles, much nicer than the Norman Palace. Sitting there he suddenly to pray privately asked his god for the forgiveness of all his prior sins. He there he climbed up to the roof of the Cathedral to admire the beautiful panorama of the whole city.

He then walked to the Quattro Cantri and saw the statues of the kings of Palermo and then walked down the street on Via Maqueda to the Massimo Theatre. The theater today is hosting world class operas. Michael then went to the Foro Italico a large public garden by the sea to take a break and walk through the trees on the sea walk. It was now about four PM and he headed straight for the Palazzo Gangi. It is the place where the "Leopard" movie by Luchino Viconti was filmed. The Gangi family still lives there, and the

Palace is preserved in all its splendor. He is amazed at the beauty of the ballroom which in the famous ballroom scene in the movie. He questioned the owner about the family tree and whether the Gangi in his family might be related. No connection could be determined.

Since it is now late in the afternoon Michael went down to the Osteria Dei Vespri Restaurant for dinner which is in the corner of the Palace. For starters he ordered Boneless quail, with celeriac puree and Marsala reduction. For his pasta he ordered Anelletti (small pasta with octopus "maiolino raou") served with wild fennel saffron of Corleone and Nero d' Avola wine. For the main dish he selected pork saltimbocca, sage and peppers, black pork lard, herbs, glazed shallots and sauteed chicory. For dessert he got hot Cassatas with ricotta cream from Gangi, with chocolate flakes and lemon reduction. He consumed a half bottle of 2016 Perericone e Nero d' Avola, Rosso del Conte Reserva. Michael was surprised to see the largest wine list he had ever seen.

After dinner he returned to his hotel and relaxed from the long day. At about nine AM he called room service and requested a night cap of his favorite perfect Bourbon Manhattan on the rocks to be sent to his room. When it arrived, he tipped the waiter and took his drink to the balcony. He sipped it while he watched the city lights of Palermo sparkle like jewels in the night.

The next day he checked out, picked up his Fiat and continued his personal tour of the Island. He drove southeast to Monreale where his grandmother was from, and he stopped at the Fountain in the middle of the square where his grandfather met his grandmother for the first time. He sat down on the ledge of the fountain and watched the towns people come and go fetching water. A beautiful young dark-haired lady walked up carrying an urn on her shoulder and placed it under the fountain to fill it with water. Michael visualized his grandfather's encounter with his grandmother. in the same manner. He then left the Fountain and visited the Cathedral and the cloisters He took pictures of everything so he could send them to his parents.

He then proceeded south, passing the wheat fields and orchards to the town of Pioppo where his grandfather was from. He stopped at a roadside produce vendor and bought an orange to quench his thirst. Along the road he passed a painted donkey cart carrying wood. Again, he was reminded of how his grandfather took exotic wood by cart from Pioppo to Palermo to sell it to the artisans.

From Pioppo he back tracked toward Palermo and took the road west to the town of Erice.

CHAPTER 24   ERICE SICILY

It was now about one PM and Michael was hungry, so he drove to a hilltop restaurant called Trattoria Visio Mare. It had a great view of the Mediterranean and he sat under a tent-like roof with a slight cool breeze blowing from the sea. He was handed a menu and it is an extensive menu with dishes that he never encountered. He can't wait to taste the food.

First, he ordered a glass of their local white wine and an Antipasto Misti platter which consisted of: - Ensalada Polpo (Octopus salad)

- Capanata Di tonnino (Italian Eggplant salad)

- Copo con Pesciolino

-Cappucetto fried Pepata di Cozzi

For his second course he selected Spaghetti Alle Siadz, pistaccchio e uvto. His final dish is Fried Calamari. For his dessert he ordered Sabeito al Limone. When he finished his typical Italian lunch and enjoyed the view, he left the restaurant and drove southwest to the town of Messina.

After Lunch he went site seeing and visited the castle of Venus at the top of Mount Erice. In ancient times Erice was known for its temple where Phoenicians worshiped Astarte, the, Greeks, Aphrodite, and the Romans Venus. At night a large fire lit the sacred area and served as a beacon. The famous Venus Ericina became the protector.

His next visit is to the Turret Pepoli, the Mediterranean Lighthouse of peace. Built by Count Agostino Pepoli between 1848 and 1911. It5 was the meeting place for men of culture, artists, and scholars. He then visited the Polo Musseale A Cordici. It is a former convent of the Franciscan Friars Minor. Named after Antonio Cordici. It contains archaeological finds such as historical -artistic, weapons, contemporary art, and a space for temporary exhibits.

It was getting late in the afternoon, so Michael headed out of Erice and drove southwest to Marsala.

CHAPTER 24   MARSALA SICILY

As Michael drove to Marsala he passed many acres of vineyards with hundreds of rows of grape vines in bloom, waiting for the grapes to emerge. He opened his window to smell the aroma of blooms. As he drove into the city the streets were paved with glimmering marble lined on both sides with ornate baroque buildings. He finally reached his destination, the Hotel Carmine on Piazza Carmine16, a three-star hotel.

It is a three-story white stucco building with a carved wooden baroque doorway entrance with an iron balcony over the large carved wooden front door on the second floor. He parked his car and entered the building. He walked into the arched high ceiling lobby and to the ornate registration desk. There is a young man and young woman at the desk and the said (In Italian) welcome to hotel Carmine.

Michael Said "Grazia" and booked a room on the third floor with a view and a balcony. The room was kind of rustic but well equipped with a double bed, desk and chair, a divan, a private bathroom with walk-in shower and toiletries, whit terry cloth towels and bathrobe.

The room also had a full screen TV, telephone, mini bar, and Hi-Fi. The hotel had a great archway well stocked Bar and cocktail lounge, with brick and stucco arches rising to a wood beamed ceilings. It also has a convenience store and a coffee shop on site. Michael found out that the young woman at the front desk is the Concierge. Michael unpacked his clothes and hung them on the cloth racks provided in the room. He then went down to front desk and asked the concierge if a restaurant with good local cuisine could. She recommended "Lei Sole" which is close, a three star and Sicilian specialties. She gave Michael the address and he said "Thank you.

It is a small intimate place right on the water. When he entered the place, he was greeted by a hostess that led him to a small white clothed table by a big window. The room was small, welcoming, and rustic with a modern touch. His seat at the window table overlooked the beautiful view of the sea and Egadi islands.

The menu was extensive, so it took him some time to select his dinner. In the meantime, he ordered a carafe of Local white wine. He then started with a Caprese salad with Bufala mozzarella cheese, tomatoes, and basil. dish of dried Ousiata with Sicilian seafood. Then he ordered Lei Isole red prawn from Viazaro, Swordfish slice, and grilled squid. For dessert he selected a crunchy cannolo with sheep ricotta cheese and orange sauce and a glass of 2011 De Bartoli padre della Vigna Passilo di Pantelleria.

Michael returned to the hotel after dinner and thanked the young lady at the desk for a great suggestion. She said "Prego" and smiled. He then went to the bar and got himself a nightcap of his perfect Bourbon Manhattan.

The following morning after breakfast he decided to Rent a bicycle that the hotel could provide. He is going to take a bicycle tour of the city. This would accomplish two things at the same time. Daily exercise and site seeing. He cycled through the street all the way to Stagnone Islands to visit the salt pans and the processing of sea salt. He took pictures of the white stucco windmills disbursed among the islands. From there he traveled on the road Porta Nuova through the ancient city center to Porta Garibaldi. He visited the iconic churches, squares, and the famous city gates. He then traveled to the Marco De Bartoli winery and vineyards to Tour their facility and taste their wines. As he drove through the white pillars and iron gates of the vineyard, he entered the courtyard of a typical 18th century farmhouse and multiple outbuildings. His drive there was flanked by acres and acres of grape vines growing Muscat, Bibbo and Grillo, and red Pignatelli gapes.

His tour took him to a special field surrounded by a five-foot stone wall. It had grape vines and a special open area with two five-foot rows about 300 yards long of white grapes lying on a white mat and two rows of red grape lying on white mats. The grapes are drying in the sun. He then toured the facility, wine cellars and the tasting room where he tasted all the wines made at the winery. The winery is about 12 kilometers from his hotel, so his ride back took him about a half hour.

He went straight to his room and took a shower and then dressed for dinner. He left the hotel and took a taxi to a second restaurant that was recommended "Le Caserie." Michael walked through a large oak carved door into a large orange brick arched tunnel like room. There are tables on the left and right side of the room and a bar at the end of the tunnel. It is dimly lit and beautiful table setting with white tablecloths.

The waiter handed Michael the menu and led him to a small round table. Michael thought this would be a very romantic setting if he had a companion for dinner. He was ready for another great meal.

He started off with the Atelier of the sea (Crispy basket with fisherman's salad and cream of vegetables scented with mustard, tuna tartare and berries. scampi, Etruscan bruschetta, swordfish marinated in ricket wine and citrus.) He then ordered Pres Pappardelle (Al Ragout of Sicilian Boar with cherry tomatoes, porcini mushrooms and basil.) For his second course he selected Baked Lobster Au gratin, with orange bisque. He had a carafe of local Nero d' Avalo.

For dessert he ordered a Cannoli and an espresso. The dinner took over two hours and Michael was in his glory. When he got back to his hotel, he thanked the concierge and went to his room and went to bed watching TV.

At seven AM the following day Michael rose and went for a run through the streets of Marsala and ran along the waterfront for the fresh breeze coming off the sea. He was in that special zone that comes with running. He returned to the hotel and to his room, took a shower and then went down to the buffet for breakfast. He packed up his things, took the elevator down to the lobby and rolled the baggage cart with is bags to the front desk to check out. The bell hop helped him out the door and Michael gave him the ticket to fetch his car.

Five minutes later his car is delivered, and he put his bags in the car and drove off. He started south with his next destination of Agrigento. It is about 84.9 miles and will take him two and a half hours.

When he reached about halfway the road turned south and east and to the shore.

CHAPTER 25   AGRIGENTO

Arriving in town, he drove to the Hotel villa Athena. A small luxury hotel set within olive groves in the valley of the temples. He booked a Deluxe double room. It has a terrace that overlooks the temples, desk, sofa, mini bar, safe, and coffee maker. The bathroom is outfitted with terry cloth skippers, and bathrobe, and toiletries.

It was now late in the afternoon, so he went to the bar and got his afternoon Prefect Bourbon Manhattan on the rocks, after which he went to his room and got in his PJ's and sent for room service to send him something for a light dinner. He then watched some TV and then went to bed.

At Seven AM the next morning he got up, had breakfast sent up to his room and sat on the terrace and ate his breakfast overlooking the city which was slowly coming alive with the hustle and bustle of the natives and tourist. He then went to the fitness center for one hour work out, returned to his room, took a shower, and dressed.

He then left the hotel for a site seeing tour of the Valle dei Templi. (Valley of the temples) which is in walking distance. The area was a Greek settlement 2500 years ago and contains extensive remains of Greek temples. He walked among the olive groves to visit the Temple Concordia which is beautifully perched on a ridge and is the most preserved of the Greek temples. As he walked to it, he passed a toppled bronze statue of a giant Greek Man. He then walked over to an olive tree that must be hundreds of years old at the foot of the ridge and then up the slope to the temple. He then visited the Temple of Herakles (Hercules) which is the oldest of the temples still standing with its 13 plus columns.

His last site is the Temple of Zeus, which now is now only a jumble of large stones, but one was the largest known Greek Temple in the World. Seeing the extensiveness of the run prompted him to visit the museum which has a recreation model of the Temple.

Michael, on his way back to the hotel walked through Giardino della Kalimbetra, the ancient olive and citrus garden. When he arrived at his hotel, he got into his swim shorts and bath robe and went down to the pool a swim. He then sat on one of the lounge chairs and got a cool drink and snack delivered to him at poolside, where he spent the rest of the day. About Four thirty he returned to his room took a shower and dressed for dinner.

It is a balmy beautiful evening, so he walks to the restaurant Accademia del Buon Gusto. A waiter with a towel over his arm and menus in his hand greeted him and seated him in the lighted garden under a big white umbrella among the exotic bushes and trees. The table is set with a white tablecloth, glasses, and table ware.

He started off with Cilindro Di Polpo(Tentacles of octopus, with crunchy celery, cubes of potatoes, quenelle of black olives Taggiasca, emulsion of extra virgin oil and sweet garlic.) He then got a plate of Le Busiate (Fresh pasta with green broccoli cream, pork sausage, stracchino cheese and Grana Padano.)

For his second course he selected Stinco di Maialino. (Low temperate cooked pork shank with red wine, cream of goat butter and reduced sauce) For dessert he ordered a cup of double espresso and Rivisitazione Cannolo. (Ricotta cream with shavings of Modica chocolate and fragments of Cannoli with coffee and candied cherries) He consumed a half liter of local red wine with his dinner.

He then walked back to his hotel and up to his room. When he entered his room, he opened the drape to his terrace and looked over the valley of temples all the various temples lit up. It was an enchanting site to see. The following morning after breakfast he checked out of the hotel and

drove to the next destination his itinerary Ragusa.

CHAPTER 26   RAGUSA

On his way to Ragusa he passed Sicilian vineyards, farms, and green rolling hills of olive groves. He drove into the narrow he drove over cobble stone streets up the hillside to the center of town. He reached his destination at the Palazzo Delgli Antoci and checked into a deluxe double room with a balcony.

The hotel has a shared lounge, bar, restaurant, coffee house and fitness center. His room as a desk, mini bar and a balcony overlooking the city and the garden. After he unpacked, he went down to the bar and had his afternoon cocktail of a perfect Bourbon Manhattan on the rocks and sat at the bar watching the guests in the room.

After about an hour he decided to go to dinner to a place called Camuri. He walked into a small garden courtyard to the entrance and a Maître di met him at

_____

the door and asked him if he wanted to sit inside or outside. It was a typical Sicilian balmy evening, so he chose to sit outside. He was then led through the restaurant to a door in the back that led a garden with whit umbrellas and preset white tablecloth tables.

Michael ordered grilled and smoked octopus with chickpea cream and salmoigano for an appetizer. Pasta with white lamb ragout, truffle oil and fondue of Tmma Persa cheese for his first course and then Rack of lamb, grilled Savoy cabbage cream and sauteed mushrooms. A bottle of 2018 Mile e una Notte, from a local winery. For dessert he selected a cannolo stuffed with ricotta cheese, and pistachio and orange marmalade. And a cup of double Espresso. He then returned to the hotel.

The following morning, he checked out and drove to the 14th century Castllo di Donnafugata. He toured the lavish halls, the hall of mirrors, smoking room, music room and the royal bedrooms. He then took a stroll through the beautiful gardens. Michael then left the castle and headed east to Siracusa.

CHAPTER 27   SIRACUSA

When he reached the city, he turned south to the island of Ortiga which now actually connected to the mainland by a filled in road called the Umbertino bridge. He drove to the Grand hotel Ortiga which is situated on the west corner of the island and overlooking the Marina and the sea. He was met by a bellhop, and he turned over his keys to his car to him to have it parked. He checked into a deluxe double room with a balcony and a view of the Marina and the sea. He unpacked his clothes and place them in the wardrobe in the room. It is early in the day, so he decided to take in some the historical sites of the city. Visiting Siracusa is like taking a trip a thousand year back in history.

His first site is the Teatro Greco (Greek theater) Michael sat on one of the stone steps and imagined hearing the echoes of heroes of the great Greek tragedies such as Agamemnon. Medea, or Oedipus. It is preserved so well that even today it is a place where a Cycle of classical Greek performances take place every year. He only wished that he could have been there to experience a performance.

The next location is the Legendary Ear of Dionysus a famous cave shaped like an ear at its entrance way. It has exceptional acoustical properties that amplify sounds on the inside. Legend has it that the tyrant Dionysus kept his prisoners in the cave and secretly listened to their discussions. He walked into the cave and tested his voice with the echo sound.

It was about lunch time, so he proceeded to the Ortiga Market located at the entrance to the island. He browsed the many tents and vendors and came across a guy shucking oyster and selling them with a free glass of wine. So got a dozen eat them and drank the free wine. He then came across among the many fresh fish vendors a place that offered a cooked fish platter of a variation of fish from the area also with a free glass of wine, so he sat down at one of the many tables under white umbrellas and ate the fish and drank the wine. He then stopped ate a fruit vendor and bought a peach and consumed it while walking and looking at all the artifacts being sold in the market.

He then visited Castello Eurialo one of the largest and complete military works of the Greek period. Built by Dionysius to complete the grand defense system known as Mura Dionigiane., the walls that run along the entire edge of the Epipoli plateau. Although there was much more to see it was getting late in the afternoon, so he returned to the hotel and went straight to the rooftop terrace bar and go this perfect Bourbon Manhattan on the rocks and sat at a small table on the terrace overlooking the city and sea. After enjoying the sunset falling over the Baroque buildings and his drink, he moved inside to a table in the Teraza Sul Mare restaurant. He now had a growing appetite and ordered his dinner.

For starters he ordered Pan roasted Octopus with ginger flavored carrot cream and olive breadcrumbs. He then selected "Mancini" pasta with sweet & sour vegetables squid and girgentana goat robiola cheese sauce. He then got a Double cooked pork fillet with pumpkin in pomegranate & green apple sauce. He then ordered a small platter of 5 historical Sicilian cheeses, served with jams wine, honey and wine. If that was not enough, he got a classic cannolo 'Aretuseo' and double espresso. He drank a half liter of local wine. He then left the restaurant and took the elevator down to the third floor to his room.

He spent another day site seeing and relaxing in his room and then went to bed. The next morning, he put on his sweats and took the elevator to the fitness center for a workout. After an hour he took a swim in the pool and then went to his room to take a shower and dress. He packed up and went down for a typical Sicilian breakfast. E ten fetched his bags and checked out. The bellhop got his car and brought it around to the entrance way. He then helped Michael put his luggage in the car. Michael tipped him and said "Grazia di Tutte."

Michael got in the car and drove away. He headed north on SS114 to E45 to the Auto Strada to along the coast to Catania. Arriving one hour and nine minutes later.

CHAPTER 29   CATANIA

When Michael reached the city, he drove to the shore and to the Grand Hotel Baia Verde a 4-star hotel built on Lava rock on the natural bay. He booked a deluxe room with a balcony, overlooking the sea. The room had couch and easy chair in a small sitting area near the balcony, a double bed, desk and chair, mini bar, safe and closet. The bathroom has all the of the features of a four-star hotel, bathrobe, slippers, walk in shower and special toiletries. The hotel has a gym, outdoor pool on the cliff with a view of the sea, bar and restaurant with a terrace overlooking the sea.

Since it was still early in the day, he took a trip to the famous Catania fish market. (La Pescheria), located in the square. He watched with interest from above at the many fish vendors yelling at the top of their lungs, competing with one another to get attention for their fresh fish specials of the day., He then walked through the upper-level streets and vendors selling all kind of fish and street food. He ate some fried fish, an Arancini and some Gelato as he walked along.

After a couple of hours, he returned to his hotel and relaxed at the pool until 4 PM. After which he returned to his room and dressed. It was time for his afternoon libation, so he went to the bar at the terrace level. He got his favorite perfect Bourbon Manhattan on the rocks. The bartender did not know what Michael meant by perfect, so he explained how to make his drink. He sat there enjoying the view of the sea with the yachts sailing by and the cool breeze from the water, while he sipped his cocktail.

About Forty-five minutes later he moved into the L'Oleadro Restaurant just inside the terrace doors. He selected the special menu of the day which consisted of:

> -Tuna tartare, with chives, ginger and soybeans.

> -Gnocchi, Vesuviana, with tomato sauce, mozzarella cheese, onions and olive.

> -Marinated and grilled beef with rosemary, dressed with carrot, fennel and pomegranate

salad.

-Cassata and espresso coffee -And half-liter of Mt Etna red Sicilian wine.

Finishing dinner, he returned to his room put on his PJ's and watched the Italian TV, and then bed.

The next morning, he got up at Seven AM, dressed and went to the buffet breakfast. His plan for the day is to visit Mt Etna which is a six-hour ordeal. He called and hired a private tour guide who picked him up a 4W drive vehicle at his hotel and drove him up to 6500 ft up the mountain. There they got out of the car and hiked through the Valley del Bove, a horseshoe depression 3280 feet in depth. Moon like dessert and landscape facing the Ionian Sea. He then was given a helmet and they explored a Lava cave. The guide gave him the history and commentary about Mt Etna the most active volcano in Europe and in the world. It was an exhausting but interesting day and the guide drove him back to the hotel.

Michael took a shower changed his cloths and decided to go to the "Flumen", which was recommended. So, he took a taxi there. He ordered an antipasto of to dinner. Crispy Baccala, roasted pepperoni, and olive oil. He then ordered a dish of pasta with sword fish, followed by seared tuna with blood orange reduction and caramelized onion. He chose a classic Sicilian Cannoli and a double espresso for dessert. Once again stuffed and having consumed a half liter of white local wine he was ready for his return to his room at the hotel.

He went to bed and caught a good night's sleep. The next morning, he went to the gym for a one hour work out and then for a swim in the pool, after which he dressed and went to breakfast. He then packed his things and checked out. When his car was delivered to the front door, he put his thing in the car and drove off to Taormina his next destination. It was a short trip of only about 45 miles and only took him about an hour.

CHAPTER 30   TAORMINA

Reaching the city Michael proceeded up the hillside to 60 Via Leonardo Da Vinci and the hotel Villa A Ducale. It is a small luxury boutique hotel perched on the elevated hillside above the center of town. When he arrived through the stone column Gate, he was met by a young man who opened his car door, welcomed him, collected his bags and keys and led him to the front desk where there is a young woman and another young man. He checked in to a Deluxe double room, with a sea view terrace. Again, it had a mini bar, safe, and private Bathroom with walk in shower, bathrobe, slippers and luxury amenities.

He unpacked his things and then opened the drape and sliding door to the terrace. He walked out on to it and saw the fantastic view of the bay of Giardini Naxos with numerous white boats anchored in the bay. To his left in the distance, he could see Mt. Etna with smoke rising from its crater.

It was still early in the day, so he decided to walk down to the old town. He descended the 600 stone steps along the high stone wall on the left and low stone wall and raw iron fencing on the right, which lined along the pathway into town. He visited the Greek theater ruins for about 30 minutes and took pictures. He then walked to the Fountain in Piazza Duomo, with its Greek statue.

His interest peeked when he stopped at the ruins "Naumache" (Gymnasium) in the area of Giarinazzo. It is a rectangle perimeter, surrounded by four sides in an area supported by 4 pillars. The clearing in the center was used for games, gymnastics and exercises. It is where Olympic athletes trained. He then walked along the street, Corso Umberto, with quaint shops and cafes. He stopped at one and got an Arancini and glass of wine for a snack to carry him over before dinner.

He then ascended back the 600 steps back to his hotel and took a swim in the pool. When he climbed out of the pool and walked over to his pool chair where his robe is, he noticed a good-looking Brunette had taken a chair next to his. She smiled as he took his seat and Michael said, "Hi beautiful afternoon isn't it" "She smiled and said "Yes, it is" She was wearing a white bathing suit with a long white shear garment over it. Michael struck up a conversation and found out that she is a model from Milan on a holiday.

It was now cocktail time so he asked her if he could buy here a drink and she said yes. So, he got his Perfect Bourbon Manhattan on the rocks, and she got a Vodka Martini. She said "My Name is Gina, I was getting a little bored, glad I met you. Michael took advantage of the remark and said, "Would you like to accompany me for dinner?" She responded that would be nice." "Good meet me in the lobby at Five thirty" with that they both left the pool and returned to their respective room.

He showered, dressed in his designer jeans, turtleneck shirt, boots, and leather jacket. He sat on the terrace and watched the sun dropping over the landscape and, a red glow and smoke coming from Mt Etna's crater. The Town below and the buildings along the waterfront started to sparkle with the evening lights.

At five thirty Michael paced nervously in the lobby waiting for his date, she walked into the lobby at precisely the right time. She was a knockout, dressed in silver, tight, short cocktail dress, silver high heal shoes and a silver tiara on he heads, and er long hair folded up on her head.

As she reached Michael he said, "You look terrific Gina." (He thought she surely is a model) They waked together out of the hotel and Michael's car was waiting for them outside. The doorman opened the door for Gina, and she got in. Michael then got in the driver's seat, and they drove off. Michael said I made a reservation at the Otto Geleng restaurant a Michelin starred restaurant." That sounds great, I have heard of that place, and that it is difficult to get a table there."

About 15 minutes later he pulled up to the ancient Baroque building and parked the car. They were seated at one the eight tables on the terrace. The terrace is adorned with Bougainvillea, and a metal trellis covered with purple flowers. Their table overlooked Taormina, the bay of Naxos, and Mt Etna. The city sparkled with all the lights from the buildings.

It was a very enchanting atmosphere.

When the waiter came to their table he asked if he could get them something to drink. Michael asked, "Would you care for some Champagne?" she responded, "Yes the would be fine." m, Michael then ordered a bottle of Don Perrier.

They both decided to order the Chef's tasting menu with wine pairing, which consisted of:

- Octopus, fried bread with pepper, broccoli, olives and vinegar pearls.

- Prawns, caviar, chestnuts, baby onions, and pomegranate.

- Spaghetti with roasted peppers, oyster, sea dust.

- Lamb with carrot, cabbage and star anise.

For dessert they were served Mascarpone with persimmon, coffee and lemon.

During dinner she told Michael that she regrets that they had not met sooner. It would have been a better vacation for her. They left the restaurant and returned to the hotel. When they got there, she asked Michael if he would like to join her in her room for a night cap. He said yes and they took the elevator to the third floor to her room. She went the mini bar and pulled out two small bottles of Cognac, then got two glasses and some ice and said "have seat on the couch I will be right back. She entered the bathroom, flipped off he shoes, disrobed and put on her shear night gown over her flimsy nighties.

She sat down next to Michael and said Thank for a great evening and she reached over a planted a kiss square on his lips. She lifted her glass and said "Salute." "Michael clinked his glass with hers and took a sip. He then put his glass down on the little table and grabbed her and gave her a passionate long kiss. She then grabbed his hand and led him into the bedroom. There they undressed and made intense lovemaking for about an hour. She fell asleep, so Michael dressed and left her room or his.

The next day he looked for her again at the pool, but she did not show up. She left a note in his mailbox at the desk. He found out that she had checked out and returned to Milan. Her note read:

"Grazia per una serata grat, annunuio di partire per una a sfilata di moda in due giorni venite a trovarmi a Milano un po di tempo. Gina"

He was disappointed that it turned out to be a one-night stand. He went to the fitness center and had a one-hour workout, took a shower, had breakfast and set out for some more site seeing. After another exhausting day he returned to the hotel. The weather turned hot, so he was all sweaty when he got back. He took a quick dip in the pool then showered, dressed and went to the roof top bar for a drink.

He is now hungry, so he left the terrace bar for the hotel villa Ducale restaurant. He was seated at a table with a spectacular view of the bay with all the sail boats moored in the bay. He reviewed the menu.

For an antipasto he selected red prawns and Yellow-fin tuna tartare with citrus, strawberries and toasted almonds. For his first course (Primi Piatti) he ordered, Norma fresh pasta with tomato sauce, aubergines, basil and ricotta cheese. He then ordered Lamb loin with pistachio panure and potato wedges. He selected a bottle of Zottorinoto Etna Rosso DOC- Nerello

Mascalese. For dessert he got a Connolo alla ricotta a double espresso. He realized that the ricotta cream in Sicily was made with sheep's milk which set it apart from all that he had ever eaten. He then returned to his room and relaxed for the evening. He went to bed and got up at Six AM, packed and checked out.

His next destination is the small seaside town of Cefalu. It's a small seaside village on the north coast. It took him two hours and twenty-two minutes and he arrived at Cefalu. It was recommended that he stop here for breakfast, so he stopped at the Osteria del Duomo and had their special Coffee and pastry combination breakfast. He then spent a few minutes in the adjacent piazza di Duomo and continued his way to Palermo. His trip is ending. It is about a one-hour trip along the north coast of Sicily.

CHAPTER 31 BACK IN PALERMO

When he reached about halfway to Palermo his cell phone buzzed so he pulled over to answer it. He stood outside his car looking at the sea while he retrieved his message. It read go to the nearest US Embassy and contact us on a secured phone line, Urgent. He got back in his car and drove directly to the American Embassy in Palermo. He drove up to the gate, got out of the car and flashed his ID to the guard. The guard opened the gate and Michael drove his car into the courtyard. He got out an entered the building. He went straight to the ambassador's office and requested to see her. The secretary buzzed the Ambassador and told her that Michael wanted to see her and who he is. She said "Send him in."

Michael explained that he had to contact Langley on a secured phone for instructions. She led him down the hall to a locked room and opened it for him. He went in and closed the door. There is a phone, fax machine and a copier in the room. He picked up the phone and called CIA HQ. He was connected to the chief of operations and his section chief. The section chief said, "We have an important mission for you, and I will send you all of the details by fax on the secured machine at the Embassy." 'OK" here is the number" Michael then gave him the fax number. He waited for five minutes, and the fax machine started to pump out numerous pages. When the machine stopped, he said, "OK I got it' and hung up. He placed the documents in his laptop case and left the room. He then went to the Ambassador's office and thanked her. He left the building picked his luggage and asked if the Embassy would turn in his car to the rental company. He then took a cab and headed for Palazzo Natoli hotel at 6 via SS Salvatore.

He checked in to a grand deluxe room with a view

overlooking via Vittprio Emmanuelle, a pedestrian street with noble palaces. After unpacking he sat down and opened his laptop brief case and pulled out the papers describing his mission. It contained a picture 54-year-old man with the name Nikolai Alexei, a Russian agent. Another sheet has a description of him and what he is wanted for. The sheet states: "He is a leader of a Russian backed procurement network that sources, purchasing and ships military and sensitive technology material back to the Russian Federal security Agency in Russia. He has been operating in the US for two years and left the country. He was last seen getting off a plane in Holland, which he has made multiple trips to buy diamonds and meet a Russian contact residing in Holland. He sends information via his contact who relays it to Russia. Sends diamonds back to a family member in Russia. If he is eliminated it is like cutting off the head of a snake. Thereby destroying him and the organization's ability to operate." He called the Italian Airlines and booked a flight from Palermo direct to Amsterdam Schiphol Airport for the next day.

CHAPTER 32 AMSTERDAM HOLLAND

His flight left at 2:55 PM and arrived three hours and five minutes later in Amsterdam. When he arrived, he caught a taxi to a hotel that he had chosen online. He instructed the taxi driver to take him to the Dylan Amsterdam hotel, at 384 Keizersgracht. It is a boutique hotel along the Keizersgracht canal around the corner from the 9-street shopping center.

He was met at the hotel by a doorman who helped with his luggage and led him to the front desk, where he signed in for a junior suite with a view of the canal. He unpacked his things and went down to the Bocco bar for a drink. It is a well-lit bar with a curved bar and 15 bar stools at the bar. The lounge also has some small tables and chairs and an area with a sofa and cocktail table.

He noticed that there is also a bar menu available, so he decided to order some food. He ordered 3 Dutch Oysters, some steak tartar and caviar, and Dutch Grey shrimp croquettes/vadouvan and lemon. He polished off a second drink with his bar food and then went back to his room and to bed.

The following morning, he got up at six 30 am with a wakeup call and put on his sweats to go to the fitness center in the hotel. He worked out for about an hour and fifteen minutes and worked up a good sweat, after which he returned to his room to take a shower. He dressed and ordered a breakfast through room service. Fifteen minutes later his door was knocked and he and an attended rolled his breakfast into the room.

Michael tipped him and closed the door. He rolled the cart over to the window where he ate his breakfast while overlooking the many boats sailing to and from on the canal. While he is eating his morning meal, he is thinking of how he is to accomplish his mission.

He realized that his best bet is to home in on the fact that his target visits the Diamond district often and thought this is where he is most likely to encounter him. After breakfast he rented a bike from the hotel and decided to ride it to Royal Coster Diamonds, the one of the oldest diamond dealers in Holland. He left the hotel and headed south on his bicycle non Keizersgracht to Runstat where he turned left onto Prinsengracht and then left onto Lijnbaansgracht then right onto Spiegelgracht then continued onto Museumbrug and then turned right toward Paulus Potterstraat where he turned left to Coster on the right. It was only a six-minute ride. He parked his bicycle outside with about 3 others.

He walked into the place and browsed around to see if there was anyone of interest in the place. Since there wasn't anyone, he went outside and parked himself on a bench across the street and waited. He watched people come and go but no target. Suddenly about four PM a man rode up and parked his bike outside the Coster building. Michael identified him as his target and crossed the street to follow him into the building. As Michael entered the showroom, he saw his target being escorted through a door to somewhere in the back of the building. That is where there are private rooms for dealers and jewelers can buy and negotiate with discretion. In about 20 minutes Nikolai walked out with a small leather case in his hand.

Michael followed him out and while his target was unlocking is bike to leave, Michael bumped into him and stuck him with a syringe full of a slow acting poison and said, "Excuse me sir.". Nikolai got on his bike and started to ride off. Michael followed him and began to sweat on his bike. As his target reached near the hotel Boheme, his bike started to wobble and then he passed out, had a heart attack and fell to the ground with his bike. Michael stopped and quickly retrieved the leather case and took off.

He returned to his hotel and turned in the bike and went straight to his room to check the contents of the little leather case When he opened it, it contained a small white envelope with a dozen diamonds about 2 karats each in size. He put them in the room safe and then went to the bar for a Drink. He then moved on to the Vinkles restaurant in the hotel for dinner. His dinner that night consisted of: Hamachi (Conierence pear, black olive, yuzu. Tomasu, soy, and garlic.}

Anjou Pigeon (Duck liver, sour cherry, rose, Cusco Chunco 100%.}

Wagyu A5 "Furano, Hokkaido" (Sirloin, imperial caviar, tongue, shisho kombu.}
Caramel souffle.

For his beverage he got a bottle of Chateau Puynard red wine. Following dinner, he took a walk around the corner to the nine-street shopping center.

The next morning, he watched the morning news and there is a report of a Russian Businessman having a heart attack and dying while riding his bike. He then sent an email to CIA HQ that read "Bulls' eye on target, White rose." He then dressed and took the diamonds to another dealer and sold them for $24,000 which he sent to his bank account in the US.

He decided that he would return to the US and retire from the service. So, he booked a flight back to DC. So next morning he packed up his things, checked out and caught a cab to the airport. He boarded a KLM flight in business class at 1:05 and eight hours and forty-five minutes later landed Washington DC Dulles airport.

CHAPTER 33   BACK IN THE USA

Michael hailed a taxi and took it to CIA HQ in
Langley. He asked the taxi to wait for him and he
entered the building and walked past the wall of honor
and through security. He entered the elevator and
took it to the top floor. He walked into the chief's

office and announced himself to the chef's secretary. She then buzzed her boss and told him that Michael was here to see him. He told her to let him in and Michael walked into his office.

Michael surprised the chief and said "I didn't know you were coming, but I am glad to see you, Michael. What can I do for you?", Did you get my text message?" "Yes, good job" "Well I want you to know that I am packing it in." While you deserve a retirement from service there is one last mission, I would like you to consider, and it it is here in the US"

Michael sunk down in his seat and said "What is it" "There is a Lebanon born woman and her husband living somewhere in Orlando who has targeted American and Muslim immigrants with a fraud scheme. She offers a high rate of return on investments and then does not deliver. She has operated under multiple company names and transfers her money to a bank account somewhere in the country. The FBI has asked us to try and help them. She also is a member of Salafi-Jihadist terrorist organization and is a fund raiser for them. The money she steals goes to the organization. Your primary mission is the elimination of the couple and a secondary mission is to find out their US contacts if possible." "OK I will take on this last mission and then it's then as they it will be time to stop and smell the roses." The chief smiled and said, "Thank you Michael, good luck."

Michael got up shook hands and walked briskly out the door. He hurried out the building to the taxi waiting for him. He decided to go to Courtyard Dulles airport Herndon hotel near the airport to make it convenient for him to catch a flight in the morning. After e checked in he went to the small bar in the hotel for a cocktail, and a snack. He then went to is room and called for a reservation for a flight to Orlando. He booked a flight leaving at 8:20 AM arriving in Orlando at 10:44 AM.

Michael got up the following morning at Six thirty, took a shower and then went for the free breakfast. He then took the shuttle to the airport. At eight AM he boarded the American airline plan for his trip. When seated he immediately was asked by the flight attendant if she could get him something. He said, "I would love a cup of coffee Ms." "Certainly sir." She then returned with a cup of coffee and Danish. The plane then took off and landed in Orlando two hours and 30 minutes later.

CHAPTER 34   ORLANDO

When he deplaned, it is near lunch time, so he stopped at the Cask and Larder restaurant in the airport for lunch. He ordered a Nashville fried chicken sandwich with hot honey, coleslaw, and pickle on a Brioche bun. He also got a house brewed Working man malt draft beer. After a quick lunch he proceeded to the baggage area where his luggage is waiting for him in the staging area. He picked up his bags and then stopped at the rental car area and rented a car with a GPS. He picked up his car and put the address of the Crown Plaza hotel Orlando.

When he arrived, he checked in to an Executive King room with a balcony and a view the city. His room had a granite dinning bar area with a small refrigerator, coffee maker and a microwave. His bathroom had a walk-in shower and many bathroom amenities. He unpacked and put his special spy craft items into the safe. He then went to the fitness center for a workout followed by swim in the pool. He returned to his room and studied the dossier his target. He then left his room for the Bite Bistro and wine bar for a drink. It is a bar, cocktail lounge and restaurant, located off the main lobby of the hotel.

Michael sat at the bar and got is perfect Bourbon Manhattan on the rocks. After a polite chat with the bartender and finishing his drink, he moved to one of the tables in the restaurant for dinner. For starters he got a crab dip, blended with sun dried tomatoes, topped with almonds, and served with crackers. He then ordered a 10 Oz Ribeye steak with garlic mashed potatoes and fresh vegetables. Then for dessert he got Warm apple pie ala Mode. He consumed two glasses of Predator Zinfandel wine with dinner.

Following dinner, he returned to his room and watched some TV until about eleven PM and then went to bed. He slept until six AM. He put on his sweats and went to the fitness center. He worked out on the rowing machine, and it reminded him of his days on the Princeton rowing team. He also on time on the heavy bag with his Karate strikes, and the tread mill for a half hour. It was the most extensive workout he had in some tine.

Following his workout, he returned to his room, showered and dressed. It was time to start his mission, so he decided to drive to Jama Masjid Mosque in Orlando to stake it out as a possible place his target and husband might frequent. It is only a twenty-minute drive and there is a place that he could park cross the street from the gated entrance. He sat in car until the first prayer hour and watched people arriving at the mosque. With his binoculars he homed in on everyone who parked their car and entered the Mosque. Neither or her husband showed up at this prayer session, so he waited until a later session and sure enough the husband drove up parked his car outside the Mosque and entered it.

When the prayer hour was over his target's husband left the Mosque and entered his car. As he drove off Michael followed him for about twenty-five minutes to house in the suburbs. He assumed that this maybe they are residing for the time being.

He then left the location and drove back to the hotel

and planned his next move. He decided to go to a Lebanese Restaurant called Cedars, thinking it would be a place his target and her husband might go for dinner. It had the reputation as the best of its kind in Orlando. Michael walked in and is seated at a small table in the back of the room that is set with a white tablecloth and preset with utensils and glasses. The dark-skinned waiter came over to take his order and Michael spoke to him in Arabic. The waiter is surprised and was pleased. Michael asked him to wait so he could study the menu.

After reviewing his options, he ordered the following dishes:

*Hummus with sauteed lamb and pine nuts.

*Quails Partially boneless, grilled, then sauteed with garlic, cilantro and lemon juice.

*A side of Garlic sauce, veggies.

*Baklava for dessert, with Arabic coffee.

He thought he would explore a Lebanese wine with

dinner so drank two glasses of Massa Terrasses de Baalbek red wine. The food was so good that he decided he return in the future. While he was eating his target and her husband came in and sat a table near him. Always being prepared he took out his camera glasses and put the on and took pictures of them. He then took out his pen directional recorder placed it into his shirt pocket and turned it on.

He recorded their conversation, finished his meal and left the restaurant. He then followed them when they left. They drove for the residence that Michael had followed the husband to before and entered the house. Now he is sure that this is the place that he must get into to see if he can get some information on their network. He left the scene and returned to his hotel.

On his return to the hotel, he went straight to the bar, sat in lounge and got himself his perfect Bourbon Manhattan on the rocks. While he was enjoying his cocktail, he noticed a good-looking blonde woman walked in went to the bar She is wearing a short red dress and red high heel shoes. As she sat down on a bar stool, she exposed her long legs. Michael thought he might want to meet her. Just as he was about to get up, she moved over to a Middle-aged guy with white hair sitting at the bar and struck up conversation with him. The bartender served her what looked like a Cosmos and the woman and guy finished their drink and both left together. Michael concluded that she was a woman of the evening as, they and had scored with the guy at the bar. Michael glad that he did not try to involve with her.

Michael finished his drink and retired to his room, where he put on his Pajamas watched TV for a couple of hours and then went to bed. The following morning, he went for a swim, took a shower, dressed and went down for a buffet breakfast. Michael left the hotel and drove to the site of the target house and parked nearby. He spent the morning stacking out the house. About eleven thirty AM the target and her husband open the garage door and drives their car out and shut the garage door.

He waited until they were out of site, and he got out of his car and walked briskly to the house. He had researched and studied the plans of the house on one of the internet sites and knows there is an entrance to the house in the back of the house. So, he went straight to the back of the property and to the sliding doors to the back of the house. There is good cover because the back yard is filled with trees and bushes around its perimeter. He picked the lock om the slider and entered a family room. He walked to the front of the room and into a little office. He placed a bug on the phone and then searched the desk drawers. He found a small address book and took pictures of all the pages and put the book back in its place and left the room and the house the way he came in. It only took him eight minutes and he was out an on his way back to the hotel undetected.

Back in his hotel he uploaded the pictures of the address book on his computer and sent a copy to CIA HQ with an encrypted note explaining what it is. Now he had to figure out how to eliminate them. He then went to the bar for his afternoon cocktail and then dinner. He left the hotel and caught a taxi to take him to the Cafe Trastevere, an Italian-Roman restaurant.

He was met at the door by a young lady who escorted him to a nice table in the indoor dining room. There already is a menu on the table and a candle lit in the center of the white clothed table for atmosphere. A waiter approached Michael and asked if he could get him something to drink. Michael said Yes and ordered a bottle of vintage Amarone. The waiter left and returned with the bottle opened it and handed Michael he corks. Michael smelled the cork and nodded his head. The waiter then poured a small bit of the wine and handed it to Michael, who took a sip and then approved it. Michael then ordered La Caprese. (Fresh Mozzarella, tomatoes, basil, and olive oil.

For his next course he selected Calamari E Gamberi Fra Diavolo (Calamari and shrimp sauteed in a spicy red sauce and tossed with Linguine.) He ordered a Cannoli and a double espresso for dessert. Michael finished his meal and paid his bill and left the restaurant for his hotel. He realized it was close enough to the hotel, so he walked back to it. It gave him an opportunity to walk of some many calories he had just consumed.

It was an unusually cool evening, and he enjoyed the walk back with the multicolored lights bouncing off the buildings in town. When he got to his hotel, he took the elevator up to his floor and walked down the hallway to his room. He opened the door and there was an envelope on the floor that had been slipped under the door. He picked it up and closed the door. He walked into his room and opened the envelope, and it was a note from the desk to tell him that he had a package at the desk.

Michael went down to the desk to pick up his package and took it to his room. He opened it and it is an assassination kit, containing a pistol with a silencer, a vial with a lethal drug, a small brick of plastic explosive and a detonator. Michael put it all in his room safe from further use. He then changed into his pajamas, read he daily newspaper and retired for the evening.

The following day he got up at six AM and worked out at the fitness center for an hour, then returned to his room to shower and dress. He went down for breakfast and then returned to his room to pick up the items from the Assassination kit and put them in his backpack. He then picked up his car and decided to drive to house of the target for a stake out.

He arrived at about seven AM, and parked in his selected spot where he could observe the house. At Eight thirty AM the couple opened the garage door and drove out of the garage. As they drove away Michael followed them. They drove about a half hour out of town to a remote area of Florida. They turned off the highway and turned left onto a dirt road about 200 feet and stopped at a Rustic cabin on a lake.

The couple parked their car and entered the cabin. Michael got out of his car with the brick of explosives and his Pistol with the silencer. Under cover of the trees on the side of the dirt road he ran and crouched behind the target's car. He then places the explosive on the under belly of the car and waited for the target come out of the cabin. When they did, he waited until they got in their car and started down the dirt road. He then pressed the button of the detonator. The car blew up with a tremendous blast and sent a column of black smoke to the sky.

The noise of the blast alerted the people in the cabin and two men came running out started to run toward the blast.   Michael instinct kicked in and he immediately concluded that they were coconspirators, so he jumped out of the bush he was hiding in and shot both men multiple times. He Then ran to where he had parked his car got in and drove away. When he hit the highway, he sped away back to the city. When he returned it was about lunch time, so he ordered room service and ordered Cheeseburger, French fries and a chocolate Milkshake. About fifteen minutes later there's a knock at his door and his lunch is delivered.

He reflected on the day before and was sure that he had eliminated multiple threats and he can now retire from the clandestine world. After all he is pushing 50, and his once black hair is starting to turn gray. Although he keeps in shape he is no longer at the top of his physical game. He called CIA HQ and told them that he had accomplished his task and that he is now going to retire. He told them to send him the appropriate forms FedEx to the hotel and he would sign them and return them. He decides that he would stay at the hotel for another two weeks for a much-needed rest.

During that time frame he saw on TV that his favorite candidate for the presidency was going to hold a rally in Orlando at the airport the next day. He decided to attend the rally in person and mad sure he got there early so he could get up close to the candidate. The crowd as overwhelming and the sea of people were all chanting USA USA and waving political flags with the candidate's name.

CHAPTER 35   THE FINAL HOORAY

As Michael is listening attentively to the various speeches he waits for the introduction of the candidate. Suddenly he is introduced, and the crowd goes wild. The candidate takes the podium and speak for about an hour being interrupted by applause about 25 times. At the conclusion He waves to the crowd and starts down the steps from the podium. Just then a guy close tom him pulls out a gun and aims it at the candidate. Being close, Michael jumps into action and grabs the guy arm and points it to the sky as it goes off. He then hit the guy with a Karate chop and sends him to the ground where the police apprehend the would-be assassin. As the police are hand cuffing the suspect, Michael disappears through the crowd.

He returns to the hotel and feels elated that he was able stop the guy from shooting the candidate. (He thought to himself that it took an assassin to stop an assassin.) For rest of the two weeks, he relaxes and when the retirement papers arrive, he signs them and returns them to CIA HQ. He then checks out and drives south to the Florida Keys. On the trip down he reflects on his life, loves, study, travels, and his experiences. He is a wealthy but lonely man and regrets not having lived a more normal life.

He arrives at his favorite island in the keys and seek out the beach house he once lived in. It is abandoned and all boarded up just as he left it. He contacted the owner and purchased it for $50,000 dollars. He then went to town and purchased some secondhand furniture and moved in. Three weeks later with slightly overgrown beard, cut down jeans and a bandanna around his head Michael spends his time walking on the beach picking up seashells, enjoying the sunsets, glimmering over the water. He sits in a Buddha position facing the water in meditation watching the sun drop below the edge of the water. The moon is now out, and Michael rises, performs a Kata with his shadow in thew moon light.

Michael spends the rest of his life as a loner, immersed in Zen, the arts and the martial arts alone with only his memories of love, and a life filled with mystery, danger, a world traveled and a head full of memories!

The End!

Made in the USA
Columbia, SC
27 August 2023

22178587R00124